Passage

of

Time

By

R.W.K. Clark

This is a work of fiction. All names, characters, locales, and incidents are
the product of the author's imagination and any resemblance to actual
people, places or events is coincidental or fictionalized.
Published in the United States by Clarkltd.
Po Box 45313 Rio Rancho, NM 87174
info@clarkltd.com

Edition 1

United States Copyright Office
#TX 8-347-416 November 2016
Library of Congress Control Number: 2017907160
International Standard Book Numbers
ISBN-10: 0997876727
ISBN-13: 978-0997876727
ASIN: B01MQW0S2V

/200801

CONTENTS

ACKNOWLEDGMENTS

I dedicate this novel to my wonderful readers and for all the amazing people I've met and those I haven't. To my family and loved ones, all your support will not be forgotten.

This book was made possible by reviews from readers like you.

Thank you

R.W.K. Clark

CHAPTER 1

1943

The Boston University campus was always beautiful in the early fall. Leaves blew all around, and an ever-so-slight chill in the air made the temperature ideal for students who were rushing about to their classes on foot. It was a wonderful college in a wonderful city, and he always felt more than blessed to be able to attend school there.

Calvin Cooper was one of those rushing students. He was headed for the science laboratory to do some research for one of his first assignments of the year. It focused on putting together a topical solution that would effectively smooth aging skin and rid it of wrinkles. He chose the topic himself, due to his major interest being ways to slow down the aging process. It was Calvin's dream to find out how to bring the curse of aging under control, to harness it, and to reverse it completely. Calvin wanted to change the world someday.

It was his second year at Boston University. He fit in quite nicely, as long as he was in the lab, but of course, there were other subjects which he was required to take to get his degree, and in those, he stuck out like a sore thumb. Calvin was good looking enough, with wavy black hair and light blue eyes. But the truth was that he couldn't be bothered to comb his hair most of the time, and his lack of motivation in this area left his peers with the impression that he was somewhat wild and antisocial. Not to mention the fact that when it came to socializing, he was not endowed with the gift of gab, and he struggled to make friends.

But he didn't care. Friends were not on the top of his list of priorities. He had no time for college parties or chasing girls. He had other things, more important things to focus on, by a long shot.

Right now he was studying dermatology, just so he could gain an understanding of the human body, its skin, and how and why it reacted to the passage of time the way it did. He knew he would not be a 'dermatologist.' Truth be told, he would likely go to school for the rest of his life and change his major a hundred times. After all, he was only twenty, and only the good Lord knew what kind of advances science would make regarding anti-aging in the future.

To put it simply, Calvin Cooper's life goal was to discover, or create, the 'fountain of youth.'

Calvin kept his head down as he rushed to the lab, occasionally running his hand through his unruly hair to get it out of his face, or pushing his glasses up on his nose. So intent was he—at looking at the sidewalk that he nearly crashed into a young woman at the door to the science building. His books and papers flew from his hands and scattered, as did the bag she was carrying and the belongings which were inside of it.

"Oh, Lord," Calvin said in a nervous and panicky voice. He stood and began to frantically pick up his books and papers, taking no notice of the girl on the ground before him. Finally, when he had his things together, he looked up slightly to see a pretty young blond trying to stand up from the ground. Her skirt was smeared with dirt, and the hem was torn and hanging down.

"Oh, I'm so, so sorry! Did I do this?"

Calvin bent over and took the girl's hand, and she gave it to him eagerly. Once she was standing, she began brushing the dirt from her skirt, then she looked around at her things. They were scattered as well, but she didn't have nearly as much stuff to gather as he did.

"I guess I didn't see you," the girl said to him as she began to stuff her things back into her bag.

Calvin kicked nervously at a rock on the ground. "Same here. I'm really sorry. I didn't hurt you, did I?"

"No, no," she said to him. "I'll be fine, I'm sure."

He began to fidget and look nervously at the door to the science building. He didn't want to seem rude, but he was anxious to get to work. He turned to the girl to make sure she was okay one last time, and that was when he really saw her.

She was stunning. Her face was round in shape, with a perfectly elfin chin, and her blond hair framed it in golden ringlets that could have easily been mistaken for spun silk. She had the bluest eyes, the color of the sky, and they shone out of her face like the light of day in the darkest night. Her cheeks glowed pink with good health, and her tiny body was perfect, in all the right places. Suddenly, Calvin couldn't think or even breathe. He stood in shock, groping helplessly for the right words to say to the angel standing before him.

"I'm Elaina," she said softly, breaking the ice as well as his reverie. She was looking at him somewhat expectantly.

Calvin breathed a sigh of relief, which made her smile a little as she held out her hand to him. "I'm... I'm Calvin. Calvin Cooper." The two shook hands, and then Elaina set about putting her bag on her shoulder.

"Well," she said. "I better be going. I'm new, and this is my first day. I'm not exactly sure where the mathematics building is."

Calvin snapped to it right away, then. "Oh! It's that building there! No problem." He turned and gestured to a building behind him. "You were almost there anyway."

Elaina stood looking at him as if waiting for him to say or do something. She maintained the smile on her face patiently as she looked him in the eye with expectation. Suddenly, Calvin caught on, and he felt his face flush with embarrassment. He gave the door to the science building a fleeting glance, then turned his attention fully on the pretty girl he had just met.

"I can walk you over there if you'd like." While he was anxious to get to the lab, he also wanted to spend just a bit of time with the girl.

Her smile broke into a full-blown toothy grin, and with dismay, Calvin felt his heart skip a beat in his chest. If her personality were half as tantalizing as her appearance, he knew he was in big, big trouble. He found himself suddenly trying to concoct a reason why he might need to visit the math building.

Elaina linked her arm through his own in a presumptuous manner which she made seem cuter than anything else. Calvin had never been so nervous; he was aware of his hands shaking, so he stuffed the free one into the pocket of his trousers so she wouldn't take notice.

"What do you study?" She asked him as they began the short jaunt to her destination.

Calvin's shoulders immediately squared off with pride. "Science is my main area of interest, but I am taking several courses to back up my main goal. How about you?"

"Education," she replied simply. She shifted her bag on her free shoulder. "My family moved here to be with me after I graduated high school. My mother couldn't bear to be so far. We are from Indiana, and she would have worried herself sick."

Calvin nodded with understanding. "That's quite a move for an entire family, especially since you are the one attending college. What does your father do?"

"He's a criminal attorney."

The two fell into silence, mostly because Calvin was at a loss for words. Elaina was gently gripping his upper arm as they strolled, and he could swear her hand was burning directly through his jacket. Her touch made him tingle all over.

He glanced over at her just in time to catch the sight of the wind blowing through her soft, blond hair. She was still smiling, and she was looking all around, taking in everything she could see. He observed her taking a deep breath, and for a fraction of a second, she closed her eyes as if to memorize the scent of the air. His heart skipped a beat, and for the first time in his life, Calvin Cooper realized he was stricken, and it had happened just like that.

All too soon the pair was standing in front of the mathematics building, looking at each other as if both were waiting for the other to say something. It was all too obvious that both of them were nervous, but they were both so wrapped up in the moment that neither noticed the anxiety of the other.

Finally, Calvin spoke. "Here we are," he said with a chuckle. "See? Not too hard to find at all."

Elaina crossed her arms over her chest and nodded at him. "If it's not too much to ask, maybe you could give me the grand tour of the campus sometime. It may just keep me from getting lost. I mean, I do have other classes, and I would hate to be late for any of them just because I didn't know the way."

Calvin knit his brow in confusion. "Didn't you get a tour at orientation?"

Elaina laughed. "Yes, but it can be hard to remember those things when the time comes to actually recall the information. Besides, maybe I was trying to come up with an excuse to see you again."

"You want to see me again?"

She reached out and slugged his arm playfully. "No, silly. I just don't want to get lost." Elaina began to turn away but then turned back to him suddenly. "Maybe we could make a day of it and have sandwiches and sweet gelatin for dessert."

With that she turned and walked away, disappearing into the math building without as much as a backward glance. Calvin stood with his mouth open, watching her dainty little walk and hoping she would turn around. He even debated whether or not he should call out to her. How would he get ahold of her to give her the tour she had requested? After all, he didn't even know her last name.

Suddenly, he jumped slightly and looked down at his watch. "Oh, my," he said as he turned on his heel and headed back to the science building. "My word, how I hate to be late!"

Calvin walked quickly to the lab, trying to get there before anyone else had the opportunity to beat him to it. After all, lab use was spared on a 'first come, first served' basis, and typically, Calvin saw to it that he was always first. But most of the time, there were not too many other students so dedicated to the subject to fight over the lab with him anyway. Deep inside he knew he was worrying for no reason at all.

For the rest of the day, Calvin tried, unsuccessfully, to clear his mind of all thoughts of the wonderful Elaina. More often than not, however, he discovered that he was distracted by her. She had swept him off his feet, and he would be sure to be waiting outside the math lab until he met up with her again.

∞

Elaina Newton found her class easily enough once she was in the building. She checked in with her professor and found a seat near the front. Other students chatted casually with each other, but Elaina's mind was not on her surroundings, or what people were saying. She was thinking about the young man she had just met; she was thinking about Calvin Cooper. She thought about the way his blue eyes set off his jet black hair. She wondered if he had a girlfriend, and then she thought not. He was a nervous wreck around her; she couldn't imagine him being a lady killer by any means, and he was a bit corny, or 'off the cob,' as her friends in Indiana would have referred to someone like him. But she didn't care; she thought he was about as brilliant as they could ever come.

She had always been attracted to those who were the more studious type. She wasn't sure why, but she thought it might be because they had goals, they focused on them, and they worked to achieve them. Not like those that hung around at the soda shop, whistling at the girls and checking out each other's cars. Calvin seemed just like the sort of boy she was attracted to, that was for sure.

But regardless of her favorable thoughts towards the handsome boy, she decided right then and there, sitting in class and listening to the endless drone of her professor, that she wouldn't overdo it in any way. She had no intention of playing it 'easy.' If he gave her a tour around campus, it would be because he called her and asked her to join him on a guided tour. Otherwise, Elaina would simply put her personal desires and daydreams out of her mind. Eventually, she would learn her way around, with or without the assistance of Calvin Cooper, the aspiring scientist.

∞

Distracted by Elaina or not, Calvin did some of his best work that day in the lab. He had been working on a face cream which was to be slathered on the face and worn at night while the user slept. It would harden into something that resembled rubber, making it easy to peel off in the morning, and it would dramatically reduce signs of aging in facial skin. At least, that was the plan.

Until that day. He had been struggling with the formula. Oh, it did have a great effect on bags and wrinkles, but he couldn't seem to get the substance to the point where it would set the way he wanted it to. The cream base didn't seem to want to set into a peelable mask like it was supposed to. He had been doing some serious focusing on the chemical makeup, and what needed to either be added or eliminated to get the mask where it needed to be.

That day he finally got it. It came to him hard and fast, and he had to give credit to that cute little blond. He made a mental note to find her and thank her, because if he became famous, it would be her doing.

Initially, Calvin had simply made the mask to be

washed off. The ingredients used were simple items which could be found in any household, with the exception of his own personal creation, which he had lovingly named 'Silkex.' The Silkex compound had been proven, thus far, to significantly reduce the puffiness under eyes and facial wrinkles and bagging, though it did not eliminate them completely. That didn't bother Calvin; with hard work and perseverance, he fully intended to discover the secret and master a formula for lifelong youth and health before the end of his life. He intended to leave a very attractive corpse when his life was over.

So, Silkex was, until that day, used in a paste-type mask which had to be washed off of the face after treatment. The thing he didn't like was the mess it made when being washed off; it turned into a sludge which was slimy, and it seemed nearly impossible to cleanse away without making a mess of everything around the user, including the user themselves. So, Calvin had been focusing, for months, on creating a mask which, when dry, could simply be pulled off the face easily while providing the same beneficial results as the 'mud' he had already developed.

He had tried everything from natural rubber-base to an extract in a new type of putty that had been developed for governmental use. But it was safe and non-toxic. Nonetheless neither of them had reacted well with Silkex, and more than once Calvin had sat up at night with his head in his hands, the glow of his desk lamp heating his hair and skin as he tried to work out a solution in his mind. He had even tried to use a mild glue that was popularly used in elementary schools, but the problem of slimy sludginess had always remained.

The day he met Elaina, before the actual encounter, he had been practically running to the lab, his mind focused on the problem to the point that he had been oblivious to all that was going on around him. He had walked her to the math building, they had parted ways, and then he had made a mad dash for the lab, and just as he entered, something that cute little girl said had smacked him in the face like an armful of textbooks: gelatin. She had mentioned having sweet gelatin for dessert.

It was so simple he couldn't believe he had missed it, but it always had been the simple things which evaded Calvin the most. Elaina had made that off the cuff comment about lunching on sandwiches and sweet gelatin, and he heard her, but he had nearly tossed it out of his mind. When it did hit him, it hit him hard, and he dove in right away. He even had one of his professor's student aides hold down his area of the lab while he ran into town on his rickety bicycle to purchase the gelatin.

From there, Calvin spent the rest of the day working up a formula, and sure enough, it had worked as though it had been meant to be. He missed the rest of his classes that day without even thinking about them, but it didn't matter. When his new mask proved to set the way he wanted it to, all he could do was sit and stare at the small pile of peelings on his table, stupefied by the fact that he had missed it. But he was thankful beyond words, thankful that he finally got it.

He finally got it thanks to Elaina. How long would he have been struggling for the key if he hadn't have run head-on into that girl that day? He couldn't wait to track the girl down and tell her. She would get her tour, and she would get her lunch. Calvin Cooper discovered that he could hardly wait.

CHAPTER 2

Calvin stood before the mirror in his dorm room fidgeting nervously with his bowtie. He never had been good with things like ties and lapels; he had always done very well with lab coats, though. Now was no exception, for the thing hung like a misshapen rag around his neck.

After another few moments, he finally threw up his hands and looked at his pocket watch: he had to leave in only three minutes if he was to be on time to pick up Elaina for the award ceremonies. He turned in a panicked circle, looking around to make sure he had everything, then left his room hurriedly, hoping against hope that she would be able to fix the demon-possessed bowtie for him. It continued to flap and fly around his face as he rushed out, running and scrambling as he always seemed to be doing.

It was a brisk and refreshing evening. Calvin walked with a pep in his step and a smile on his face. Not only was he receiving Boston University's Student Scientific Achievement award for his Silkex mask, but he was also taking the most beautiful co-ed on campus as his date to the ceremonies. Yes, things were going even better than he could have hoped for in his life, and if he had his way about it, things were only going to get better and better.

The co-ed dormitory where Elaina boarded was about ten minutes across campus, and Calvin had plenty of time to think. He considered his mask formula, which not only accomplished its purpose but the rights for which had also been purchased from him for a considerable sum by a pharmaceutical company, to be a dismal failure. Sure, the mask worked, but only if it was used on a daily basis, and the smoothing appearance it provided faded by afternoon. He just wasn't satisfied with something so temporary.

He wanted a lasting youthful appearance to be the result, but Calvin Cooper wanted much more than that. He wanted to achieve youth for the entire person, inside and out, and he wanted it to really, really last. That, of course, was going to take a lot more than Silkex and gelatin. It would take years of hard work, focus, experimentation, and further study. He would have to find the missing element that would accomplish his goal.

Men had been searching for the very same thing since the dawn of mankind. He was not one to fool himself. If he was going to achieve his dream and make history, he didn't have time to waste or play around.

He would graduate this year, and he would be taking the money he made from his Silkex mask and open up a private laboratory. There he would set his focus on his true goal, and he would work on it tirelessly until he found the solution or solutions he was looking for. But that wasn't where his planning stopped.

He would also ask his steady girl of six months for her hand in marriage. Elaina Newton had not only been his companion, but she had also been his primary inspiration. She had been the light of all his days, and some of his evenings as well. Calvin couldn't imagine spending his life and chasing his dreams with anyone else.

She was the perfect girl for someone like him to marry. She was supportive, loving, gentle, and kind. She was the kind of girl a man needed if he wanted to succeed. She would be a friend and a helpmate. Even if she wanted to pursue teaching, he was okay with that. Just to have her at home was enough for him.

He turned the last corner, and a smile came over his face as the exterior lights on her dorm building hit his face. She would be waiting for him in the lobby area; he could see her tiny little self, sitting on the settee, waiting for him with her itty-bitty purse and her spotless white gloves. Yes, Calvin would ask Elaina to be his wife, and he would do it tonight, directly after the award ceremonies.

He entered the building and signed the guest book in the foyer before stepping into the lobby area. Just as he had imagined, there sat Elaina, looking as if she were literally on the edge of her seat. When he crossed the threshold into the lobby, her blue eyes immediately lit up, and she quickly stood. The vision she presented to him took his breath away immediately.

She wore a white satin, form-fitting dress that was

slightly bunched at the breast. It was sleeveless and had dainty black crocheted roses embellishing the scooped neckline. Instead of white gloves, she wore black and black patent leather heels held her dainty feet. Her hair was up in a fancy bun, and delicate wisps framed her face. In her hand, she held a small black patent leather clutch.

"You look like a vision, Elaina," Calvin told her in a low voice, his cheeks flushing as he spoke. "I cannot believe a woman like you would agree to attend anything with me, much less something as formal as this."

She blushed as well, her lashes fluttering. "I was hoping you would approve. Thank you, and I wouldn't have it any other way, Calvin Cooper."

Calvin kissed her cheek and offered her his arm, which she took with pride on her face. The other girls in the lobby giggled absurdly, but neither he nor Elaina paid them any mind; to him, she was the only female on the face of the Earth. He couldn't be more proud that this was the girl who he would share his evening with, or that she would hopefully be the one he would share the rest of his life with. As far as Elaina was concerned, all of those catty females were just jealous, and she loved it.

As soon as they got outside, Calvin asked her, "Um, I'm a bit embarrassed, but…"

"You would like it if I would help you tie your tie?"

Calvin flushed a deep red. "How did you guess?"

"Well," she replied, "It's been flapping around your

face since you walked in."

He looked down at her as she tied it, her little purse tucked under her upper arm. In only a couple of short minutes, she had it looking perfect, though he couldn't see it. He knew she would never let him go to such an event looking like a homeless ragamuffin.

The award ceremony was going to be held in the on-campus banquet hall, which meant another walk for the couple, but the night was fine, and neither of them minded a bit. Elaina had brought a light black shawl which she had Calvin drape over her shoulders, and they strolled to the event at a nice pace. They kept their conversation light, and their steps were even lighter.

"I am so very proud of you, Calvin," Elaina began. "Who would've thought when I met you that I was in the company of a genius who was already making a name for himself?"

Calvin chuckled. "I didn't think it, that's for sure."

"Well," she continued, "I can hardly wait to see what the future holds for you."

Right then he was nearly overcome by temptation. He nearly spat out his proposal right there, but he managed to keep control of himself. He did stop and turn to her, a slight smile on his face.

"Elaina," he began.

She stopped as well and looked up at him, her eyes lit up with fondness. "Yes, Cal?"

His heart was pounding, and his palms even began to sweat. "I just want you to know how much I care for you, and I hope you are indeed around to see my future, as I long to see yours."

She smiled at him lovingly, and then he grabbed her arm once again and abruptly, the two continued walking, but no more words were exchanged for the remainder of the walk. Soon, they were climbing the stairs to the banquet hall. Music wafted out from inside, the sound of the college band echoing in the night. It seemed like a dream to Calvin before they even entered the building.

Once again, for the second time, he stopped, right at the door to the building, and looked down at Elaina. "Thank you for coming with me. You look wonderful; you will outshine all others."

She smiled at him, her perfect white teeth glimmering. "And you should know, Calvin Cooper that you are the most handsome man I have ever known. Thank you."

Together, arm in arm, they started up the stairs for the banquet hall.

∞

"Scrutiny and discovery are the cornerstones of science," said Professor Edwin Berg. "Our first award tonight recognizes these things clearly. The award for Boston University's Freshest Discovery goes to Harold Wright!"

The massive room broke out in applause which was nearly deafening. Harold Wright was a junior who was majoring in biology, and he had managed to identify a brand new breed of insect which was closely related to the praying mantis. To identify any new species was a claim to fame for an aspiring scientist, and the young man's acne-riddled face was glowing with both pride and embarrassment as he made his way to the stage to accept his award.

His speech was short and stuttered. He would go down in textbooks, and he would finish out his time at the college getting more dates than he ever had in his life. The only person he thanked was his mother, and then he skittered off the stage as quickly as he had taken it.

Professor Berg returned to the podium and began to shuffle through his papers. The room was quiet as the man cleared his throat and made a light joke to fill in the gap. Calvin's mind wandered to the wonderful meal they had been served: veal with almond crusted green beans and roasted baby potatoes. Wine and champagne were readily available for those old enough to imbibe, and dessert had been a choice between lava cake or cheesecake. Calvin smiled as he recalled how Elaina had gracefully skipped that course. She knocked him off his feet.

"And now we will recognize the more creative side of science," the professor finally continued. "Necessity is the mother of invention, as we all know, and we have some of the most creative students on the planet here at Boston U. The following award recipient invented a bicycle, but not just any bike. This one allows the operator to take a friend or loved one who uses a wheelchair on bicycling adventures safely and comfortably. The award for the Most Practical

Invention is being given to George Huber for his 'Wheel-a-Chair'!"

More thunderous applause erupted as the fresh-faced and slightly bulky George strolled to the stage. Calvin knew George to an extent, and he was aware that the man's appearance was a wonderful mask for the levels his ego would soar to. He was cocky and overly self-confident, but Calvin assumed it was a major contributing factor to his success in his field.

True to form, George's thank-you speech was far longer than the first. He discussed the dire necessity for an invention such as his, and he managed to thank everyone from Adam and Eve to President Truman. Calvin caught himself yawning and covered his gaping mouth with his hand more than once, which appeared to entertain Elaina immensely. She elbowed him with amusement and fluttered her eyelashes when he blushed. When George began to show signs of wrapping things up, Calvin immediately snapped to full awareness, and his hands began to sweat. He was up next; the final and most important award of the evening was his. He wanted to be fully ready, for he didn't want to embarrass himself or his date by stumbling over his feet or his tongue.

Elaina reached over and clasped him affectionately by the hand. He turned and smiled at her, but he could see by the look on her face that she was aware of exactly how nervous he really was. She gave him a strong, reassuring smile, then delivered a wink. Calvin took a deep breath and looked at the stage just as George finished, and the audience started the nerve-wracking applause once again.

Professor Berg walked back to the podium once again, this time ignoring the papers which were sitting atop of it. He offered the audience a brilliant smile and began to announce the final award.

"And now, I am pleased to be the bearer of glad tidings!" he said. "The Scientific Achievement Award is Boston University's most prestigious award for science, and it is given in recognition of the student who has not only shown incredible dedication but who has proven his worth in the field through the development of a product which is beneficial and desired as well as having the potential to hold future promise development-wise."

He paused for dramatic effect and looked around at the large audience. "The recipient of this year's award has studied tirelessly, I might add, the effects of aging on the human body and has successfully managed to develop a formula which has proven to treat the physical signs of aging on human facial features. I am also very proud to say that he has sold his formula for great profit and will be opening a private laboratory upon graduation, so that he may continue his studies and his work on a more intense basis."

This year's recipient of Boston University's Scientific Achievement award is Calvin Cooper!"

So intense were Calvin's nerves and thoughts as he stood on shaking legs that he didn't hear one clap, but as he looked shyly at those around him, making his way out of his row to the aisle, he could see them clapping with great fervor. He wondered how he couldn't hear them, and it made him feel a bit strange. He walked to the stage on a cloud, floating as if in a dream.

As Calvin neared the stage, the fog began to clear from his ears, and the applause began to creep in, increasing in loudness with each passing second until he thought it would overwhelm him and explode his heart. He reached the podium with trembling hands and legs, and flashbulbs began to pop in excess as he reached out for the professor's hand. As they shook, Professor Berg handed him his framed award.

"Smile for the camera, Cal," the professor shouted over the applause.

The man turned and smiled perfunctorily, then Berg stepped back and gestured for Calvin to step up and give his speech. As the applause slowly died, he looked down at the award with his name emblazoned in fancy calligraphy. When he looked up, the applause was over, and hundreds of people were looking expectantly back at him, waiting to hear his words.

He looked out at the audience, a smile flittering over his lips, his eyes darting to and fro as flashbulbs continued to burst. What should he say? Hadn't he memorized a speech? Did a speech matter? No, he would say what came to mind, and he would keep it brief.

"I have loved attending Boston U," Calvin began. "I love science, and I love helping people. Boston has nurtured both of my loves and given me the tools I need to improve the quality of life for others, primarily in the field of anti-aging. I am committed to continuing to learn as much as possible to assist others in looking and feeling as young as possible, thereby bringing them health and happiness.

I will only thank my fellow science students for their support, and finally, I will thank my love and best friend, Elaina Newton, without whom Silkex would never have come to be. Thank you."

Applause exploded yet again, and the flashbulbs began popping once more. Calvin shook Berg's hand another time, then turned to make his way off the stage and back to the peace and serenity of Elaina's company. Soon there would be mingling and dancing, drinks and laughter. After that, he would take Elaina out to the solace of the bench under the willow tree, and hopefully, she would allow him to put a ring on her finger.

When the crowd began to stand and make their way into the ballroom, Elaina touched him gently on the arm. "Excuse me, Cal. I'm going to visit the powder room, okay?"

"Sure," he replied with a nod. "Meet me at the bar in the ballroom, okay? I'll be waiting for you." He smiled and nodded briefly.

Elaina squeezed his arm and gave him an affectionate peck on the cheek before disappearing into the swarming crowd. Calvin turned to make his way to the ballroom, and he made it about twenty feet when suddenly someone grabbed his arm and spun him around. He nearly tripped over his own feet with surprise.

"Calvin!"

It was Clara Gibbons, a brash red-haired business student who was far more interested in marriage and money than in management. Calvin had taken her out twice in his first year: once to a campus party and once to a diner for coffee. She was an abrasive, loud personality with a reputation for being loose. After their coffee date, he had a difficult time shaking her and her affections. She had followed him around, slipped him silly notes, and had even hung around outside the science building waiting on him, and that had lasted for two months. Finally, Clara had drifted into another hemisphere, and Calvin had nearly died from the relief; she was definitely not the girl for him.

"Clara," he replied, his eyes searching the room for any sign of his Elaina's return. "Good to see you. How have you been?"

The girl linked her arm through his and began to steer him through the ballroom door. "Great! The bee's knees! How about giving me the first dance, huh? I can't believe your award! You've done so well!"

She continued to lead him in the direction she wanted him to go, but Calvin wasn't even paying attention. He was looking anxiously around him as she rambled on; he was trying to spot Elaina, but they were getting further from the bar and close to the dancing. His mind began to race nervously. What if he lost track of Elaina due to the annoying girl who was steering him mindlessly into chaos?

The band was blaring, and Clara was shouting over the music. Calvin turned to her just as she threw her arms around his neck, quite literally hanging on him. She was gazing at him and smiling.

"Dance with me, Cal," she shouted.

Calvin took her by the upper arms to remove her, and just as he was getting ready to decline, she stood on her toes and planted a long, leisurely kiss on his mouth. He didn't kiss her back, but his shock did not permit him to pull away, either. Suddenly he looked around, her lips still locked onto his, and that was when he saw Elaina, staring, wide-mouthed, at both of them.

Elaina turned and ran, bumping into people and stumbling over her own feet. As Calvin ripped Clara off of him, the girl began to laugh. "What's wrong, Cal? Are you afraid your love and inspiration won't LOVE you anymore? Shame!" Her laughter seemed to turn into an evil cackle.

Her laughter sickened him, and he ran off after Elaina as quickly as he could, but she was fast, and he lost her in the crowd. He wound his way through the mingling guests, his heart pounding and his head beginning to ache. His thoughts were filled with panic; he knew that Clara had done what she had done on purpose. She had behaved so brazenly just to exact revenge for him not seeing her anymore. He felt firm hatred towards the evil little vixen; she was everything he hated in a woman.

He was nearing the main entrance now, where he assumed Elaina had gone when he was stopped by

Professor Berg and a couple of his colleagues. "Calvin! Son, I want you to meet Dr. Conrad Foster. He's—"

But Calvin put his hand in the air. "I'm sorry, Professor Berg. I'm going to have to catch you in a bit. Excuse me, gentlemen, please. I don't mean to be rude, but…"

He pulled away and forced his way through a group of men and women conglomerating with champagne at the main door. When he pushed it open, he was met with a blast of cool air, which took his breath away. He ignored it and ran out into the middle of the yard, looking here and there for his precious Elaina.

People were all over the place, some strolling, some chatting, but Elaina was not among them. Calvin barely took notice of any of them, though. He looked frantically around the yard area, his eyes jumping from person to person. Where could she be? Certainly, she didn't try to go back to her dormitory all by herself, in the dark of night?

Finally, he began to walk around as he looked, hoping she was simply walking off her shock, anger, and hurt. He went around the far left side of the building, but there was only one couple there, and they were making their way to the parking area at the rear of the building. He then followed them to the rear, only to see cars starting and people preparing to leave. Calvin took a deep breath, and his shoulders dropped.

He decided to go back inside and grab his award, then head to the small courtyard to the right of the banquet hall. That was the place he had intended to propose, and it was there that he would sit for a minute before heading to Elaina's dorm building to find her. He could only imagine how it had looked to her when Clara pulled her stunt, and the thought caused his anger toward the conniving girl to begin to build once more.

He retrieved his award, politely excusing himself from all who tried to stop him to chat in the process, explaining he had gotten separated from his date. Then he made his way to the side stairs and the exit located there. He didn't want to have to deal with everyone and explain the truth behind why he was leaving. He just wanted a minute to gather his thoughts and get to Elaina with ready-prepared words of explanation and apology.

Once again he entered the chilly night air. There was a sidewalk which led into a small thicket of bushes and trees, and it came out into a wee clearing which was surrounded by the same. In the clearing was a stone bench which had been dedicated to a deceased alumnus of Boston U, and it was flanked by breathtaking rose bushes. He didn't expect them to be in fresh bloom, of course, but he was hoping for peace and quiet for a few minutes, even if he couldn't lose himself in their aroma.

He came into the clearing, which was lit only by the hazy moon, but he could clearly see that the area was already occupied. He stood squinting in their direction with a heavy heart; he simply couldn't get a break, it seemed. Perhaps if he waited, quietly, for a moment, the person would leave, and he could take their place.

But then the person moved. There was something

about the way they held their head and shoulders which tugged at his heart. The person sitting on the stone bench wasn't simply some stranger. No, it was exactly the girl he had been running around searching for like crazy.

"Elaina?"

The girl turned to him abruptly, and though the moon was at the back of her head and he couldn't see her face, he knew immediately that it was she. She was sitting there, right where he had wanted her to be sitting, only she was alone. There was no one else in the area at all. The relief which Calvin felt had a tangible quality, and he exhaled audibly.

He rushed over to her, and Elaina stood just as he reached her. She was clutching her shawl around her shoulders as if the chill of the evening was getting to her. As he neared, he could see by the look on her face that she was both confused and unhappy.

"I didn't expect you to come out here," she said to him.

He smiled in the faint light. "That's funny because this is precisely where I had planned that we would come."

She turned from him and took a few steps before turning back to him once again. "Who was that girl? The red-head with all that makeup?"

Calvin sat on the stone bench, his eyes focused on her entirely. "She was a girl I dated only twice during my first year here," he said. "She turned out to not be my type at all, and I had a difficult time shaking her attention, but tonight was the first time I have spoken to her at all in a very long time, Elaina."

She didn't respond. She just looked at him and waited for more, so he continued. "Actually, she laughed when she saw you. I think she intended to cause us to quarrel from the beginning. She even made a joke before running off. She really is quite the... bother."

After only a moment of hesitation, Elaina joined him on the bench. "Really?"

"Really."

"Why would someone do something like that?" she asked.

He shrugged. "Because she isn't even a sliver of the woman you are, my sweet Elaina."

Satisfied, Elaina pulled her shawl tighter and looked up at the moon. Calvin draped his arm around her to share his warmth. She looked down and noticed his award lying on his lap.

"How do you feel?" she asked.

Calvin chuckled. "So much better now."

"Me, too, but I meant about the award, silly."

He clucked his tongue. "Oh, you mean this silly thing." He lifted it and waved it absently toward the sky. "It's nice and all, but I am a far cry from accomplishing the things I have in mind. Speaking of which, if I am ever going to meet those goals..."

He handed her the plaque to hold, which she took without question, then he stood and rummaged through the pocket of his trousers, but only for a second. Then he knelt down before her, taking note of how wide her eyes grew by the second.

"Elaina, I am going to need someone in my life who is not only my best friend, but someone who believes in me and all that I do," he began. "I believe you are that person." Calvin opened a small box he was holding in his hand and held it out to her. "I love you with my entire being, and I simply cannot imagine my life from here on out without you. With all that being said, would you be my wife?"

Even in the dim moonlight, Calvin could see the tears pooling up in her eyes. Her mouth had dropped open as she looked down at the ring nestled snugly in the box. It had a beautiful diamond solitaire set in gold. It was not a massive stone, but it was not a small one either.

A smile formed on her lips, and suddenly she laughed.

"What's so funny?" he asked.

Elaina sniffled slightly and dabbed at the corners of her eyes with a dainty gloved finger. "No! No, it's not funny. It's just that I should have known you wouldn't betray me with someone else." She looked him in the eye. "You bet I will be your wife!"

With shaking hands, Calvin removed the ring from the box. He took her by the tiny gloved hand and slipped the ring right over the cloth. "The only time you had better take this off is when you take off these gloves. Then you need to put it right back on… got it, lady?"

"Indeed I do," she replied shyly.

Calvin sat back down on the bench and put his arm back over her shoulders as she admired the ring on her finger. They kissed, right there in the chilled evening. When they were finished, he said, "Now what?"

She turned to him, her grin sly and wide. "Now we go back in, have our dance and our drink, and show Miss Sassy Red-head who's boss!"

With that, Calvin Cooper and the future Mrs. Cooper both laughed heartily, and together they walked hand in hand back to the banquet hall.

R.W.K. Clark

CHAPTER 3

Calvin stood at his workstation in his laboratory. He was using a scalpel to cut minute pieces from a variety of food items so he could continue researching the proper mix for his youth formula. For the last ten years, he firmly set his focus on his dream, and he had managed to discover that very specific natural foods had powerful cleansing and revitalizing properties. Calvin was convinced that extraction of specific chemicals from these foods, then the subsequent mixing of the proper amounts of each, would take him to the next phase of what he liked to refer to as his 'forever' pill.

Right then he was cutting samples from blueberries, red grapes, and Brazil nuts. He had already extracted a large variety of compounds from other foods, and they were currently isolated and kept cold in storage. He had already proven, to himself and Elaina only, of course, that these compounds had the potential to help him realize his dream; he had done this using rats. The issue thus far was that the amount of the compounds needed was so vast that taking his work to the next level was nothing more than a pipe dream at this time. He had to press on, because he had a very long way to go indeed.

He glanced up at the clock; it was lunchtime, and his stomach was growling quite loudly. For years, he had been eating nothing for lunch but the 'throw-outs' from his experiments: the leftovers which remained after he made extractions. The fact of the matter was that for the last few years these were the only things he had eaten. He didn't tire of them, necessarily, but when he went home to meat on his plate, he was one of the most grateful men in the world.

He grabbed up a ceramic plate off his lab table which held a sizable pile of scraps consisting of fruits and nuts, and he sat down at his desk. He began to eat, chewing slowly as he gazed out his lab window into the sunlight, and he reflected on his beautiful Elaina. Nearly ten years they had been married now, and it had been ten years of sheer bliss.

His wife was never one to nag, not about the long hours he kept or the light foods he ate. The only thing she ever mentioned was the strange habit he had gotten into of not looking into the mirror. It resulted in him wandering through life with his hair standing straight on end and his clothing looking askew most of the time. She would help him comb his hair and fix his ties each day, all the while asking him, "Why, Cal? Why?" He would simply tell her his appearance didn't matter to him; he had better things to worry about, and after all, he worked alone.

But that excuse was far from the truth. In all honesty, Calvin had a very good personal reason for dodging mirrors, though he was afraid it would seem childish and unreasonable to her: she was beautiful, and he was a bit… homely. He knew it, and every time he did look in the mirror, it would spark a fear in his soul that was unbearable. What if she left him for another man, one more handsome than he? She certainly could.

But he did trust her, and so the only solution, at least in his mind, was to avoid the fear by not looking at his reflection at all, and it worked.

He tossed two red grapes into his mouth and thought back to the beginning of their marriage. The wedding ceremony had been nothing short of thrilling to him. It was a small gathering, but wonderfully beautiful. Her parents had been in attendance, and they were thrilled with the seemingly perfect match. Calvin had no family in attendance. A few of the boys from the science program had come for him, but no family. His mother and father were strapped financially, and always had been, not to mention the fact that his father didn't care much for Calvin anyway. He wouldn't come, and he wouldn't let Cal's mother travel alone, even if Cal paid her way. It broke his heart, but it really was the way it had always been, and he pushed the memory out of his mind every time it reared its ugly head.

Elaina's parents made up for his loss, but initially, they had voiced a single concern, and that was concerning their daughter's decision to turn her back on her dream of teaching. She announced to everyone, Calvin included, that she intended to focus on the home they were going to build together. Her mother and father were disappointed, and her father was a bit perturbed over what he considered 'wasted' money spent on her tuition. They also felt that she needed something to do during the days when Calvin worked so much, which was all the time. What her parents thought of her decisions didn't matter to her half as much as her husband did. He needed her; after all, he was something of a mess.

But she was adamant. Since they had more than enough money from the sale of Silkex, Calvin tried to pay her parents back for the tuition they had invested, but they refused, and soon they came to terms with her decision. If she wanted to do nothing but care for her husband, they would not dictate otherwise. Besides, her mother had pointed out, that way they could focus on providing her with tons of grandchildren. Calvin thought it was a splendid idea.

But children were not to be for the Coopers, at least thus far. At first, they had tried and tried but to no avail. Finally, they both visited the doctor, who said they were likely never going to be able to have children. The problem was not Elaina, as far as he could tell. After extensive testing, the doctor believed that the issue was with Calvin, and he recommended that they adopt.

But, true to form, Elaina refused. She said if it were meant to be, it would be someday. She loved taking care of her husband, and that was what she wanted her life to be about. She wanted to be his helpmate, supporting his success wholeheartedly. She never seemed to have regrets about it since, and when he tried to talk to her about it, she simply waved it off. Elaina said she was happy, and unless it was causing him a lot of grief, she was willing to leave things be.

So, they lived their lives, just the two of them, in their own little private heaven. Neither ever complained; he never wanted more, and she never asked for more. They were happy, content, and very satisfied.

Calvin crunched away on the last bit of Brazil nut meat on his plate and put the plate to the side. He drank a tall glass of water to wash his food down, and then he stood and took a nice, long stretch. Time to get back to work; after all, he had much to figure out, and much to do.

∞

Elaina Cooper rapped lightly on the laboratory door. In one arm she carried a paper bag with cold chicken and a bowl of homemade potato salad, in the other she had a container of iced tea. It was ten o'clock at night, and Calvin had been at work all day. She knew he was starving, and the fact was, she was starving for his company. He tended to lose track of time easily when he worked, and her understanding of this enabled her to meet him at his level. Besides, she loved to surprise him at the lab after a long, drawn-out day. It always brought a smile to her face to see his expression when she walked in.

There was no answer when she knocked, so she shifted the things in her arms and gave the door one more rap, a bit louder and more insistent this time. "Calvin, it's me, love!" Nothing.

Finally, she set the container of tea down on the

floor and tried the knob; like always it opened up right away, so she used her small foot to hold it open so she could grab the beverage and duck inside without a problem. To the right was the actual lab, with its countertops, burners, beakers, and other essentials. It was a cluttered mess, which drove her crazy, so she forced herself to look away. He liked things the way they were.

To the right was a tattered brown sofa flanked by a pair of beat-up oak end tables. An old chest of drawers was to the left of the sofa up against the wall; it held clothing for the days at work when he had a meeting, or if he had an accident and ruined whatever he happened to be wearing at the time. She made sure it was always fully stocked for him, including hygiene essentials. Elaina made a mental note to check for dirty laundry and make sure he didn't need anything restocked.

There, on the sofa, was Calvin. He was dead asleep, his mouth wide open. His dirty white lab coat was stained with a variety of unidentifiable things: the colors red, blue, and green were smeared here and there in no certain pattern. The cuffs were smudged with what appeared to be dirt and ink, and the right side pocket held more pens than it should have, one of which had left a tell-tale dark black glob of ink on the pocket from leaking.

Calvin's glasses sat crookedly on his face, and every hair on his head seemed to stand up on end, giving him the appearance of one who had been shocked by electricity. He snored lightly, deep in sleep and oblivious to her presence. A proud smile of love curved over her lips. Even after ten years, just looking at him made her heart skip a beat. How she loved her silly, overworked man more than life itself.

She set the bag of food and the container of tea on a small table with two chairs; this is where they usually ate together when she came, though Elaina knew that he never sat there when he was alone. She removed her sweater and laid it across the back of one of the chairs before returning to the sofa. There, she knelt down next to her husband and gazed at his sleeping face; he certainly was the most handsome man she had ever known, bar none.

Elaina took a few minutes to admire his face. His long eyelashes which hid the intelligent sapphire blue eyes which he was blessed with. His black hair, which made those same blue eyes stand out so boldly in contrast. Calvin had dark circles under his eyes, and this caused her brow to crease with concern.

She took his glasses gently off his face, folded them, and laid them down on the end table at his head. Then she smiled once again, and with a soft, gentle forefinger, began to trace his brow, then his jawline and chin. Gooseflesh broke out on her skin, and she felt a rush of warm love, just as she always did when her skin came into any kind of contact with his. She leaned forward then and planted a soft, loving kiss on his cheekbone, directly beneath the corner of his left eye.

Calvin's eyes began to flutter, almost unnoticeable at first, then a bit more rapidly. He shifted his eyes in her direction without turning his head, and when he saw that it was she, he smiled broadly. He always loved the sight of her when he opened his eyes. She shone brighter than the morning sun on a clear day.

"What time would it be, Mrs. Cooper?" he asked softly, finally turning his head in her direction.

Elaina's eyes flickered to a noisy electric clock which hung over the chest of drawers. "Nine minutes past ten, Mr. Cooper."

"At night?"

She nodded, an amused smile on her face. This was a regular ritual they went through, at least twice a week, sometimes three or four times. It never angered her, only worried her for his health. She also knew that Calvin didn't eat right at all; he wasn't the breakfast sort, aside from his usual cup of coffee, and he never brought lunch to the lab with him. When she questioned him, he always told her he ate fresh fruits and vegetables at the lab, and she knew he wouldn't lie to her. In the end, she always let the subject drop. She would simply make sure he had a large meat and potatoes meal ready and waiting for him on the occasions that he did make it home for supper.

With his mind still in a bit of a fog, Calvin struggled to sit up on the sofa and get his wits about him. He rubbed his eyes and shook his head as if to clear cobwebs from both. Elaina watched him go through his normal process of waking, a smile on her face and warmth in her heart.

"Are you hungry, Calvin?" she asked as she took his

hand in both of hers and stroked it with her thumbs. "I brought supper; I thought we could eat together."

He stood and stretched out his tall frame. "I can always depend on you to take the selfless route, Elaina. Here it is ten o' clock at night, and you waited to eat just so we could do it together. You must be starved!"

She shrugged and stood, walking over to the small table. As she unpacked the food, she said, "It's no big deal. I'm certainly not dying of hunger; after all, I eat far more than you."

Calvin chuckled and followed her to the table, where he took a seat. She had brought two plates, forks, knives, and glasses. He reached for the container of iced tea and began to fill both of the glasses. "My dear, selfless wife," he stated. "Always concerned about my welfare, never concerned in the slightest for her own. What will I do with you?"

Elaina brushed him off and sat down to prepare their plates. "The question is: what shall I do with you? How are things going today? Work-wise, I mean."

Her husband was already tearing into his potato salad, and now he rushed to chew his first bite a bit faster. "Well, I guess. I should say 'par for the course.' Nothing new, but no setbacks either. I do have an appointment to interview a potential assistant in the morning. That should be music to your ears."

"Really?" Elaina was, indeed, pleased with the news. If there was anything Calvin needed, it was an assistant, someone who could aid him in his work, but still lived a bit of a normal life on a somewhat normal schedule. She hoped that such a person would give him a bit more stability in his day to day schedule. Unfortunately, he had gone through several different assistants in the last few years; they never seemed to stick around for long. It seemed that Calvin's dedication to his work almost scared them. "What do you know about the person?"

He paused, his fork halfway to his mouth. "His name is Ralph Gordon, and he is twenty-five years old. His wife recently passed away from cancer, though I am not sure what type. He worked at Bio-Labs as an assistant until she fell ill, at which time he resigned to care for her full time. Now that she is gone, he is ready to work again. I'm sure it will keep his mind off of his grief, anyway. I did some checking with Bio-Labs, and they have absolutely nothing but the very best to say about the man. They seemed genuinely sorry to have lost him, though they understood completely, all things considered."

Elaina watched him as he continued to shovel potato salad into his mouth as if it were the last he would ever eat. "That's so sad," she said in a distant voice. "Well, I'm certainly glad you may have found someone. I can tell you, I hope it works out this time."

Calvin finished the last of his potato salad and washed it down with a half-glass of tea. "He has experience in human medicines and personal cleanliness products, which makes him just the type of person I need. I can only hope he can tolerate my 'unusual' practices and habits. No one else has ever been able to, or so it seems."

Elaina chewed on a bite of chicken and glanced at her husband's plate as he stood to scrape it in the garbage; he hadn't touched his chicken, but that was not unusual. Over the last few years, he had gotten further and further away from eating meat, at least, he didn't eat it the way he used to at the beginning of their marriage. He seemed to have a preference for fresher foods more and more, and while she knew it was good for him, she thought he was simply too frail. His eating habits certainly hadn't had any negative effects on his looks, though. As he sat down again, she looked at his face and smiled once again; he was more handsome than ever. It seemed as if he looked as good as the day she had met him, but she supposed her love for him gave her that impression.

She finished her food as Calvin flipped through a 'Modern Medicine' magazine, then stood and scraped her own plate off. "What time is the interview?" she asked as she began to pack up the dinner items.

"Nine-thirty in the morning," he replied. He put the magazine aside and looked up at her. "I was thinking about staying here, but now I think I will go home with you. It will be nice to sleep next to my wife."

Elaina looked at him in surprise. "I would love that, Cal!"

He stood and moved up behind her, wrapping his arms around her waist. He planted a kiss on her neck and said, "I appreciate you more than you know, more than I show, my dear. I'm sorry I am a difficult husband."

She playfully shooed him off of her, blushing. "You are not difficult, love. You are driven. They are two different things. Every other woman could only hope for a husband as 'difficult' as you are."

"I am afraid that someday you will begin to see me for who I really am, and you shall run off and divorce me. You shall leave me for some doctor or lawyer who uses their hair treatment and a comb on a regular basis."

Elaina turned to him, faking a stern look. "I will never leave you. I intend to stay with you and make you miserable until the bitter end!"

The two laughed a bit at her joke. Once the meal items were packed up, they put on their jackets and left the lab, Calvin making sure it was locked behind them. As they walked into the darkness of the night together, holding hands, they were silent. The pleasure of each other's company was enough to satisfy them both.

CHAPTER 4

1965

Calvin stood in the middle of the bedroom which he and Elaina shared. He was staring up at the ceiling, an intense look on his face. His hands fumbled and struggled to tie his necktie, and he was frustrated, growling slightly under his breath.

The door opened right then, and Elaina popped her head in. "Are you nearly ready, love?"

Calvin's hands fell to his sides, exasperation all over his face. "As usual, the basic workings of my necktie evade me completely. Would I be a burden if I asked for your help for the hundredth time?"

Elaina shook her head, amused, and made her way across the room to her husband. "Three-hundred and forty-ninth," she stated firmly. "And no, you would not be a burden. When I signed up for this, I noticed that the tying of ties was written in the small print."

He watched his wife as she began to tie the accessory properly around his neck. She was so beautiful; he wanted her to always be beautiful and healthy. He wanted both of them to live, young and happy, in harmony. It was what drove his work more than anything, especially since the years seemed to be slipping away, out of control.

"If you would just look in the mirror now and then, Cal, you would find this task to be much simpler," she said, scolding gently.

He ignored her as he continued to gaze at her face. Finally, she finished, and she adjusted the tie perfectly, giving it a pat before looking up at him. "Happy twentieth anniversary, Calvin Cooper."

His hands went to the tie, and he gave it a good feel. Satisfied, he replied, "It's been twenty years? No! I could swear we just wed last week. You certainly don't look like a forty-year-old woman."

"And you most definitely do not appear to be a man in his mid-forties."

He put his arm around her shoulders, and the two of them left the room to put their jackets on. "I certainly hope the food at Chez Petit is as good as Ralph says it is," Calvin said. "I hope they have an extraordinary salad."

"You know, it wouldn't hurt you to indulge in a nice beef or chicken for a change," Elaina replied. "Even a fish would be satisfying, don't you think?"

Calvin shrugged as he held up her wrap so he could place it over her shoulders. "I just order what the palate wants."

In a deep, mocking voice, Elaina said, "What the palate wants, the palate gets."

"Indeed, Mrs. Cooper."

As the pair drove to the restaurant, radio playing,

Calvin thought about the last twenty years. He thought about his marriage and his work, and the progression of both. He also thought about the fact that it was 1965 already; where had all the time gone?

Time had been kind to his wife. She was still very beautiful for a woman in her early forties, especially when compared to other women her age. She kept herself well, and she was always fashionable, but Calvin could see the years on her face ever so slightly. He encouraged her to use the Silkex product he had sold years ago, and even made sure she kept it in stock at home. She thought it was silly, but she indulged him, and he thought it made her glow, but it didn't eliminate the signs of aging entirely, and that drove him even harder. She constantly sacrificed and gave, and she deserved to be beautiful forever.

But even that was not enough. He wanted to focus on his work, but he wanted them both to live long enough to enjoy as much time on the Earth as they could, and now, well, now their lives were half over. It seemed to Calvin that he would blink and it would be gone. But not if he could find the secret. Then, and only then, would he be able to stop time in its tracks for them both.

As far as work went, he had narrowed down very specific proteins and compounds from a variety of fruits and vegetables which showed great promise when combined. But there were setbacks: it took massive amounts of every formula he produced to have an effect, and this was required daily. Also, he struggled terribly to make his formulas palatable, but thus far each and every one tasted horrible. He experimented on himself only so he could vouch for the terrible tastes, and he refused to subject anyone else to them, though he did have a small group of rats who were blessed enough to sample his wares.

The problem was that it was difficult to measure the positive effects of his formulas on furry white rats. The only way to really tell if the formulas were working was through testing of their blood. He would look for changes which usually took place in animal chemistry during the aging process, but he looked for them in reverse. His work was showing promise, but it needed such a massive amount of work and fine-tuning that he was beginning to wonder if he would ever find the key.

All Calvin Cooper wanted was to maintain youth. Sure, he wanted to do it for men and women of the world, to boost their confidence and their health, but most of all he was doing it for Elaina and himself. He was doing it so they could be together for as long as possible. He wanted to be her husband for longer than the anticipated average; he wanted them to live into their hundreds, loving each other and enjoying each other's company, the way they always had.

Ralph Gordon had turned out to be the best assistant he had ever had. Ralph had been with him just under ten years now, and the two fit together like a hand in a glove. The man was loyal and dedicated, and he believed in the work Calvin was doing. He didn't mind any of Cal's strange work habits, or even his habit for completely losing time when working. As a matter of fact, Ralph seemed to appreciate the distraction. The man had no interest in finding a new wife, or any new relationship for that matter. He was satisfied to work with Calvin, taking notes, running errands, and following other necessary directives. Yes, Ralph was quite a blessing as far as lab assistants went, and Elaina treated him as one of the family. The man often ate with them during their late night meals at the lab, and sometimes even visited them at home for a meal and an evening of television. It didn't happen often, as Calvin would rather be working, but when it did Ralph fit in perfectly.

But lately, there had been a few issues when it came to working, though Calvin didn't think they would amount to anything in the end. A group of young college students had formed a type of alliance for animals, an alliance which focused on animals being treated fairly. The students rallied and protested for their cause with great fervor, and they had been gaining quite a bit of attention for their activities.

Initially, upon their introduction and for some time after, Calvin paid the group no mind. They didn't bother him, and he never really gave them a second thought, outside of brief discussions with either Elaina or Ralph when their activities gained public notice. Any effect they may potentially have on him never even entered his mind, and he didn't give the group, which was called 'Advocates For the Rights of Animals In Domestic Sciences,' or AFRAIDS, the attention they wanted. The group fought for the complete elimination of the use of animals of any kind in laboratory experimentation.

At first, the group did nothing more than march, protest, and rally. They held conferences and spoke to news programs and magazines about their cause, but other than that, they seemed like a pretty level-headed bunch of kids with an over-inflated fondness for lab rats. Calvin didn't worry; his formulas were completely natural, and so he didn't allow rumors or anything else to cause him concern when it came to AFRAIDS.

But recently, there had been a few occurrences which were very worrisome indeed. One company in Pennsylvania which produced makeup and hygiene items for women had been looted, and a fire had been set in the main lab. All of the animals in their lab had been set free, and they were found running rampant on the company's property. It had taken authorities days to gather them up, and some of them were even found dead due to exposure to the elements and local animals, like cats, preying on them.

Because of the animals being freed as well as a graphic message painted on the main wall in front of the building in spray paint, the police were convinced the incident had been the work of AFRAIDS. The message, written in blood-red spray paint, blared:

FREE THE FUR

FIRE THE FAKES.

An investigation had followed, but police were unable to pin anything on the group at all. The company building suffered five-hundred thousand dollars in damages, not to mention the negative publicity the company suffered for their use of lab animals. The business was suffering terribly, and it was thought they would never get their heads above water again.

Two more similar incidents had happened which bore the exact same signatures: one in San Diego, California and the other at a factory in Massachusetts, and to date neither had been solved. It looked like the culprits were staying a few steps ahead of authorities all the time.

But even with the events which were happening, Calvin felt no concern whatsoever. As a matter of fact, it never crossed his mind, not even once, that they may cause a problem for him, either now or in the future. He had no reason for concern.

He and Elaina arrived at the restaurant in high spirits, giggling and laughing together like a couple of kids. They sat at a romantic table for two with dim lighting and soft music all around them, and they ordered foods with strange names that neither of them could pronounce. It was a wonderful evening all in all, even though the food was not the best they had ever eaten. Both of them seemed to have American tastes at heart.

During the last half-hour of their meal, they polished off their bottle of champagne together and reflected on their marriage. They discussed how happy they had been, and how neither of them would trade their lives together for anything. They exchanged gifts to top off the night: Calvin gave Elaina a diamond and pearl bracelet which accented her tiny hand perfectly. Elaina gave him an electric shaver. She was particularly excited because she had been the one to shave his face for the entirety of their marriage due to his avoidance of mirrors. Now, he would be able to shave himself without cutting his face all up, and she was tickled by it.

The evening was perfect.

The drive home was spent in comfortable silence, the couple holding hands as Calvin navigated the roads like an expert. The radio played cheerful tunes, which they loved, and both agreed, out loud, that it was a wonderful anniversary celebration. Both looked forward to the next twenty years.

As Calvin pulled the car into the driveway, their headlights were cast over the front of the house, lighting it up in the darkness.

"Calvin!" Elaina suddenly said with alarm. "Someone is on our front porch!"

He brought the car to an immediate halt and put it in park. Both of them threw their doors open and got out, heading quickly to the porch, but the person met them in the yard before they reached the house. It was Ralph Gordon.

Elaina let out an audible sigh of relief. "Ralph! What on Earth are you doing slinking around here in the dark? You scared the living daylights out of us both!"

"Calvin, Elaina," the man replied in a breathless voice. "I have been pacing out here for an hour. There has been an... an incident at the lab."

Calvin took the man by the arm. "Incident? Wait. Elaina, take Ralph in the house. I'll turn the car off; I'll be right in."

Within five minutes, Calvin and Ralph were seated in the living room while Elaina prepared coffee in the kitchen. "Tell me what's going on," Calvin said as soon as he sat down.

"Well," Ralph began, "I had left my briefcase in the office, and there were some notes I wanted to re-read and re-write, so they were more legible for you. I went to the office, and when I got there, all of the lights in the main office area were on; I could see them through the windows, and people were moving around inside."

Calvin was alarmed, but he controlled himself, taking in everything Ralph was saying to him. "Go on."

"Well, I ran to the door and put my key in the lock, and right away I could hear whoever was in there," he continued. "They were beginning to panic when they heard my key, and they started to run around and get even louder. I had just unlocked the door and opened it in time to see the last person run out the fire exit behind the reception counter. The alarm to the door was going off, and I couldn't even think. I ran to the door, but all I could see was their backs; they were running away, and there was no way I could catch them."

Calvin stood and began to pace, as was typical for him when he was in thought. "Do you have any idea what they were doing in there?"

Elaina came into the room with a tray holding a coffee pot, condiments, and three cups. She set it on the coffee table and began to pour the coffee as Ralph continued. He was calmer, but he was still wringing his hands a bit, and his face was still flushed.

"All I can tell you is that the filing cabinets in the main area were completely ransacked; the drawers were pulled out, papers had been thrown all over, and I'm pretty sure some of the files are missing from the second cabinet," he said.

Calvin stopped and turned to him. "Missing files? How do you know that?"

"Well," Ralph continued. "I called the police, and while I was waiting for them to arrive, I scanned the mess on the floor a bit. All of the files I saw were from the second cabinet, which held the N through Z files."

Elaina offered Ralph a cup of coffee, which he eagerly took. He took a long sip, his eyes closed, then took another drink before continuing. "The drawers from that cabinet were all pulled out, and they were empty. Only a few loose sheets of paper were in the drawers. But the A through M file cabinet, well, the drawers were pulled out, but…"

"But what, Ralph?"

He took another drink. "But, in my opinion, another person was going through that cabinet, and they weren't as careless. All of the files were intact, except for the files for Laboratory Mammal Requisitions; they were all gone."

Calvin sat down hard in his chair. He was thinking hard, but more than anything he was confused. For all of his genius, the obvious was evading him.

"Why?" he asked aloud. "Why would they steal requisition files for the rats?"

Elaina put her coffee on the table and sat forward. In a gentle voice, she said, "I think the answer is obvious, Cal."

He turned to her, his face more confused than ever. "What?"

"I think it may have something to do with that group from the college," she replied. "The animal group, AFRAIDS. They must think you are doing something in the lab to harm the animals."

In seconds the confusion left his face. Yes, that was exactly who it was. But he was doing nothing to harm those rats in any way! If anything, he was helping them!

"I would never hurt them, and we all know it!" he said in an angry voice. "Who do these people think they are, anyway, that they can just break into other people's places of business and do as they please when they please?"

Ralph spoke up once again. "I'm afraid none of us know, Cal. Anyway, the police came and took a report. There had been no access gained to the laboratory area. I would say because of that heavy lock and metal door you have on them. But they took the report, and they recommended that we invest in some type of alarm system for intruders, Cal."

Calvin stood up. "Elaina, I am going to change, and then Ralph and I are heading to the lab. I want to go through things and determine exactly what was taken, that way I have a better idea of what's missing, and I can communicate better with the police."

She gave him a nod, and he strode quickly into the bedroom. As he dressed, he turned over what little information he did have in his mind. Animal requisition forms? What good were those to a bunch of activists? After all, it wasn't illegal to purchase rats for scientific use. He was angry and confused, and he felt terribly violated. At least they didn't get into the lab and steal his records and notes; that would have been terrible.

He finished quickly and headed out to fetch Ralph and get on the road. In his mind, time was of the essence. He wasn't willing to lose all the work he had done, and this puzzle needed piecing together as soon as possible.

∞

Calvin and Ralph stood in the reception area of Cooper Laboratories, staring at the wreckage that had once been highly organized paperwork and records. Ralph had been correct: one cabinet was completely emptied, its contents were thrown carelessly all over the room. Not one sheet of paper remained in its proper file.

The other cabinet stood, still full, with its drawers wide open. The only thing that was obviously missing was a significant number of files in the 'L' drawer. A large empty gap was all that remained, making it look as if a rotten tooth had been extracted in a rush.

Calvin stood, his arms crossed over his chest, staring at the chaotic mess surrounding him. He was seething with anger, and he was at a complete loss for words. It took very high levels of nerve and presumption for someone to go into the world and workspace of another human being and cause such damage and mess. But all they had taken was files. How did the police ever expect to catch them?

"What time did all this happen?" he asked, his head beginning to hurt from the stress and the sight before him.

Ralph let out a ragged breath. "Let's see, I wasn't even home when I realized I forgot my case, and I turned right around to come back and fetch it. I would say around six-forty-five, just a bit after we both left and locked up. It was just getting dark."

"What did the police do?" he asked. "Do I need to go to the station?"

Ralph shook his head. "No. They took a report, searched a bit, and looked for evidence. They said they would file the report and send a detective tomorrow to talk to you. That would give you time to look things over and see if anything else is missing, anything I wasn't aware of. The only reason they dealt with me is because I am your employee."

Calvin sat down in one of the hard orange lobby chairs. "Well, I should be thankful that they didn't interrupt our meal, but I would have rather been notified immediately, Ralph. For future reference, if anything like this ever happens again, I wish to be contacted right away, okay?"

"I'm sorry, Cal," the man replied. "I just panicked, I guess. I wanted the police to get here as soon as possible. I should have called the restaurant, but by the time we were finished with the report, it was after nine. I would have missed you anyway."

Now Cal nodded and stood up. "Yes, you're probably right. It's okay; don't worry about it. You did the right thing." He paced for only a couple of moments, then continued. "You may as well go home and get some rest. I'm going to give Elaina a call to tell her I'm staying. I'm going to start going through things and cleaning up. I need to make a definite list of all things that are missing."

"I'll stay and help, Cal," Ralph said with insistence.

Calvin turned to Ralph. "Are you sure? I could use the help, but I am sure you are tired. If you do want to stay, however, you could make a list of precisely what they took while I go through this mess."

"Absolutely. I could never leave you here to deal with all this alone."

He turned and looked at the solid metal door leading to the lab. "You haven't been in there at all?"

Ralph shook his head. "No. I'm sure they planned to break in, though. I'm pretty sure they thought they had all night; I surprised them."

Calvin pulled a large ring of keys out of the pocket of his trench coat. He walked up to the large door and inserted a key into the heavy-duty lock and turned it. Then he turned the large lever handle and hit the door with his shoulder to help him maneuver its weight. It came open, and he reached in and flipped on the lights, illuminating the room.

Everything looked to be in its place; not one item appeared to be disturbed. Calvin quickly walked to the nearest window. "Help me draw the shades, Ralph. If they had a reason for targeting us, they have likely been watching."

The men closed all the shades, then went through the entire building and checked all the doors to be sure they were secured and locked. Calvin reset the fire alarm attached to the exit the burglars had used, and soon the two men were satisfied that everything was shut up tight. Both of them were able to breathe much easier, and a lot of tension left them both.

Next, Calvin put in a quick call to Elaina. He filled her in on the state of the lab, and let her know that he would be staying to inventory the files and clean up. He also told her he would be talking to the police the next day.

"Cal, please, please be careful," she said, her voice sounding as if she were on the verge of tears. "If this is the work of AFRAIDS, well, we all know they like to set fires. I cannot bear to lose you, my love!"

He closed his eyes, his heart aching over the fact that these people had planted fear in the heart of his precious wife. "I will be fine, dear. I promise. Call me often to be sure, if you like, but I would rather you get some rest. I love you, and I am so, so sorry that we are going to be spending the night of our anniversary like this."

She readily forgave him and wished him all her love.

With that, Calvin hung up, and he and Ralph set to

work on cleaning up the mess which the crooks had left behind. The two men worked diligently and carefully, not wanting to miss anything. Cal nearly thought the requisitions were the only things missing, but just as they were nearly finished, he realized one more file was gone.

"Which one?" Ralph asked, pen poised to jot the information down.

Calvin turned to him, his eyes ablaze with anger. "The dosing schedules for my rats."

CHAPTER 5

"Since both sides have been presented to the court in their entirety, I will now call a recess until two-thirty this afternoon. During this time, I will consider all the evidence and will return with my verdict." Judge Harrison Reed lifted his gavel and brought it down hard. "Court dismissed!"

Calvin's attorney, J. Brian Nelson, gripped his shoulder with confidence. "This is going to come out in our favor, Cal. Go, have a good lunch with Elaina, okay? I'll see you back here say, at two-fifteen?"

Calvin nodded and offered his attorney a weak smile. "Sure thing, Brian."

He turned to Elaina, who was sitting behind him with the other spectators. She was grasping her purse and sitting straight as an arrow. He gave her the same smile and a quick nod before standing and walking to where she sat. "Let's have some lunch, dear."

The two left the courthouse hand in hand, and Calvin handed the keys to the car to his wife. He didn't want to drive; his body felt as if it were filled with electricity, and he didn't want any added stress.

Eight months of lawyers and court appearances had

come down to this day, the day he would receive his verdict on charges of Animal Cruelty and Practicing Scientific Arts Unethically.

The day after the burglary at his lab, Calvin and Ralph had gone down to the police station first thing the following morning, list in hand. He had expected to give the list to the police and find out what would take place as far as their investigation of the crime which had been committed against him. He was eager to get brought up to speed on the process because he wanted the criminals to pay. They had not only stolen files which were valuable to his work, but they had also set him behind by taking documentation of his progress in the form of the dosing schedules, and those papers would not be easy to replace. Nothing could fix that except more work and even more documentation.

But when they arrived, the police immediately separated the men and put them in separate rooms. There, Calvin waited for a total of three hours before anyone came to speak with him. When they finally did, the meeting went from being an owner's report and update to a criminal arrest, and Calvin Cooper was the one being charged.

It turned out that the police had been paid a visit in the early morning hours by an elementary school boy. With his book bag on his shoulder, he entered the station and stood on his tiptoes at the tall front desk, where he gave the duty officer a fat file of paperwork secured with rubber bands. Included in the paperwork were missing files from Calvin's lab, as well as photos of him dosing rats in his lab. Unfortunately, there were also photos of him disposing of two dead rats. Only Calvin and Ralph knew that those rats had been ill since he got them, and not only that, but they were fairly old to boot.

It was all very incriminating, and it was enough for him to be charged and arrested. The police even thanked him for coming down and saving them a trip to his home. The only thing they would divulge was the fact that the files came from an anonymous source; the schoolboy had been given a dollar by a stranger to take them into the police station and turn them over to the law. The police were rude and sarcastic with him from the very second he identified himself to them upon his arrival at the station.

But none of that mattered to Calvin. He believed wholeheartedly that AFRAIDS was behind the entire thing. He figured they were too spooked to return to the lab and set a fire. Instead, they made it so the law would deal with the 'murderous scum,' as an anonymous letter included in the file had referred to him.

So, he sat in jail for two days before he was finally arraigned. Fortunately, he made the bail amount ordered by his arraigning judge easily, and he was able to return home. From there, his life was a shambles, and if it hadn't been for the love of his life by his side, he doubted he would have put up a fight at all. Everything seemed to be against him evidence-wise, and he looked like a terrible man, if not a mad scientist, through and through.

The attorney who represented his and Elaina's estate and finances, Fred Carne, didn't have experience in criminal matters, and he recommended J. Brian Nelson. Nelson had an impeccable reputation, not to mention a nearly flawless track record of defense. He took on the case right away and even made it something of a vendetta to bring down AFRAIDS.

Now, here they were, eight months later, getting ready to hear the verdict of Judge Reed in only a few hours. Calvin was nervous, but something inside of him told him it was all going to be okay. He was an ethical man and scientist, and the events of the last several months had been nothing more than a setback. He was confident that he would soon be back in his lab, which had been closed up during the trial. Sure, he was a bit afraid, but he chose to be positive.

∞

He and Elaina now sat in a booth in a small café only blocks from the courthouse. Both had a green salad sitting in front of them, and both of them pushed and poked at them with their forks. The tension in the air was almost tangible. How had such an awful mess been made by people who had not the slightest idea what or who they were talking about?

Calvin glanced up at his wife. No, she was not handling this as well as he by a long shot. Sure, she demonstrated grace and determination, but the lines around her eyes were deeper than ever, and there were several gray hairs on her head. His heart broke for her;

this was taking a terrible toll, and she looked completely worn out. He made a silent promise to himself, right then and there, that he would make it up to her. He would see to it that he gave her back her youth, the youth that this case had stolen so violently from her.

Calvin put his fork down and reached across the table and took his wife's hand. "It's going to be okay, Elaina. You'll see. There will be no conviction, dear."

She looked up at him and offered him a smile, but it didn't touch her eyes. "I know, love. But even if there is, I will always be yours. I will always be by your side." She paused for a moment and looked down at both of their hands, admiring the way his strong fingers held hers so gently. "You know, those activist people went to great lengths to bring trouble on you and your work. I believe you when you say you are doing nothing harmful, either to animals or people, but they are convinced. I know that the three strangers seated in the back row belong to that group, and I can't help but wonder what is really going to happen."

Calvin smiled at his wife. "Elaina, the Lord knows that I am innocent of the charges. When we are most unsure is exactly when we have to trust Him to bring the truth into the light and see to it that the right thing is done. Don't you believe that?"

She gazed into his blue eyes for a bit before responding, and when she did, he could tell by both the look on her face and the tone of her voice that she felt better. "Yes, I do. You beautiful man. I cannot wait until this is behind us, Calvin. I want to move, to relocate both our home and the lab. Let's go someplace where we are out of the city and away from the craziness of the age, shall we?"

He didn't even have to give it thought. "I think that is a brilliant and perfect idea, my dear." He looked at his watch. "Let's eat what we can; we need nourishment, both of us. Then we can walk together in the park and enjoy the weather before we return. What do you say?"

Her reply was to pick up her fork and stab it into her salad. She lifted a large bite off the plate and put it in her mouth. When she had chewed it well and swallowed it, she said, "I'm in, Mr. Cooper. Let's face this horror and put it as far behind us as possible."

∞

Calvin sat in his seat in the courtroom waiting for his attorney to finish talking to the prosecutor. Every spectator in the room seemed to be chattering away, and the sound was very similar to that of a dull roar. He felt his nerves were highly on edge, but he was determined to not let his anxiety show. He was confident in his innocence, and the last thing he wanted was for the other side to think he wasn't. Not to mention the fact that Elaina's calmness depended on his.

Brian Nelson returned to their table and took his seat beside Calvin. He clasped him firmly on the shoulder and said, "How do you feel?"

"Good," he replied, then he shrugged. "Well, as well as can be expected, considering the circumstances." He let his eyes glance briefly toward the group in the back of the room, the trio whom Elaina had spoken of at the café. They sat quietly, seemingly the only ones not speaking in the courtroom, and glared at him with smoldering eyes. He looked away and suppressed the urge to smile at them. They were schemers and connivers, and they were not worth his time or concern at all. The only thing people like that were truly interested in was chaos and destruction, and the fact that he was dealing with this mess proved that full well.

Seconds later, Judge Harrison Reed emerged from the door leading to his chambers, a file in his hand. He stepped up to the bench and adjusted his flowing black robe just as the bailiff called, "All rise!"

The entire room stood as Reed took his seat. He pounded his gavel once and stated, "You may be seated. The court is now in session."

He shuffled briefly through his files, then began to speak, his voice somber and his expression unreadable. First, he discussed the charges and the seriousness of them. He also talked about the frequency in which companies and scientists did things that endangered people and animals in the current times. After touching briefly on that and making his stance well-known, he turned to Calvin.

"Calvin Myron Cooper, please rise."

Calvin quickly looked at Bryan, who nodded for him to oblige, then he stood and faced the judge.

"Mr. Cooper, the charges you are facing fall right into line with the examples I have just given," he began. "However, it is not your responsibility to prove your innocence, rather, it is the prosecution's to prove your guilt. On the charges of Animal Cruelty and Practicing the Scientific Arts Unethically, I must take into consideration what these mean under the law, and I must determine, beyond a shadow of a doubt, that you have committed these acts with malice aforethought.

"With that being said, I am convinced that other corporations are guilty of these acts every day. However, from the evidence presented here in this court and discussed during the trial, I must say I am not at all convinced of this in your case. Nothing in your laboratory or records which were discovered, confiscated, and brought to light was a danger to any living thing or the environment. The closest questionable evidence was in the form of photos which showed you with two dead rats. There was nothing in those photos that led me to believe you had harmed them intentionally, or in any way even accidentally for that matter." The judge then turned to the spectators, and he even directed his gaze on the three individuals in the back row. "Animals, like people, die. I believe that is likely exactly what happened in those two cases. So…"

He shuffled his file, putting it back in order, then set it to the side. "Calvin Myron Cooper, on the charges of Animal Cruelty and Practicing the Scientific Arts Unethically, I find you not guilty. Both charges will be dropped, and your record will reflect no such proceedings." He banged his gavel once more. "Court is adjourned."

Just like that, it was over.

Once again, the room broke out in chaos. Calvin

hugged Brian, thanking him over and over. Then he turned to his wife and embraced her over the solid wood partition which separated them. She was shedding tears of relief, and he took the time to hold her and comfort her. As he did so, he took note of the strangers in the back of the courtroom. They were standing, fury on all of their faces, and that fury was directed at him. They had lost, and they were not happy about it.

Yes, it was time to take his wife and his work and leave the forsaken city.

R.W.K. Clark

CHAPTER 6

1976

The decision to move to Montana, and the move itself, had gone so well that Calvin knew it had been meant to be.

After the trial ended, he and Elaina spoke to Ralph and let him know that they intended to move, then they proceeded to ask him if he would be willing to relocate as well. He was more than happy to do just that; after all, he believed it would do his heart good to leave the home he and his wife had lived in for so many years, and starting over was the best way to go about it.

Next, the three of them began to discuss where they should move to. Calvin thought that would be the hardest part of the process, but within the first hour, Elaina came up with the perfect way to narrow it down: she suggested that they throw a dart at a United States map, and where it landed was exactly where they would land.

The dart landed dead on a small town called Twixt, in the heart of the hills of Montana.

They were all happy with the outcome, and the next step was for Calvin to find them a home. The requirements they had were very specific: away from the city, but near enough to a town that it would be easy on Elaina to do the shopping, banking, and other necessary errands. They also wanted to be close to physicians and a hospital; Twixt had two doctors, but the nearest hospital was just past it in a slightly bigger town of about six-thousand called Randalia.

So, armed with plenty of statistics and information, Calvin contacted a realtor in Randalia and let him know what they were looking for. The man, in turn, mailed the Coopers photos and information on several homes for sale in the area. As it turned out, all of them but one were too close to one town or another. But the one that was not turned out to be exactly what they were looking for.

It was a four-bedroom ranch-style home situated on twenty acres in the foothills approximately fifteen miles from Twixt and twenty-five miles from Randalia. The trio decided that Ralph would have one of the bedrooms, with two more of the bedrooms serving as home offices for both men. There were three outbuildings: one was a double garage, one was an old stable, and the other was a large, brick beast that had at one time served as an office building for the horse ranch that had been on the land at one time. With renovations, that building would serve as the future home of Cooper Laboratories.

In the weeks since the trial ended, Elaina had been feeling a bit run-down, so Calvin and Ralph flew to view the property and tie up all the loose ends. The move itself took next to no time at all after packing and transporting, then unpacking, was complete. Once they were all settled in, they knew they were exactly where they were supposed to be, and it was a wonderful feeling.

Now, Calvin sat alone on the porch in a wooden rocker that he had pretty much claimed in silence. He was completely content to enjoy the alone time; Elaina and Ralph had both retired long ago, but he had not been quite ready to go to sleep. The clear Montana air and sky always seemed to help him to wind down his mind.

∞

They had lived there now for just about nine years, and a wonderful nine years it had been! In 1985, he and Elaina had just celebrated their fortieth anniversary the week before; Calvin could not believe so much time had passed. In their sixties now, Elaina was still beautiful, but she had aged more than he would have liked, especially when he considered the line of work he was in and the focus of his studies. Calvin felt as if he had made no progress at all.

Of course, he knew this wasn't completely true. Since the laboratory building had been renovated, he had been able to easily place much more focus on his work, much more than he had been able to since moving, and the fact was, he had made some improvements to his formula. He was still using protein extracts and focusing on using compounds which, prior research had proven, regenerated cells which were damaged by sickness and age. He also hadn't had to deviate far from the natural ingredients he had always used, and the best part was that he continued to waste absolutely nothing; he still ate the leftover bits that he, as of yet, had found no other use for.

He wasn't testing his youth formula on himself, Ralph, or Elaina. As a matter of fact, for the first seven-and-a-half years after his lab was complete, he continued to use his precious rats in his studies, and he was sure there were very specific behavioral differences he could positively note, but that was where it seemed to end. Their appearances did not change at all as far as he could tell, and in his opinion, that should have been the first thing to show if his formula was really working.

The more he thought about it and discussed it with Ralph, the more convinced he became that it was vital that he finds an animal with obvious physical signs of aging on which to test it. The rats were, indeed, all too young. When he had them shipped, they shipped him specimens which were lab raised and had aged very little. Yes, he needed a different, more aged test subject.

So, just over one year ago, Calvin and Ralph had been driving home from a trip to Randalia, where they had traveled to pick up a new burner and a box full of beakers. On the return trip, Ralph happened to notice a weather-beaten sign along the side of the deserted road on which they were driving. Ralph, always the chatterbox, read the sign out loud simply because it caught his attention.

"Old Mare for Sale – Name Your Price"

"What did you say?" Calvin asked, confused by the off-topic blurting.

"That sign back there, the one we just passed," Ralph replied. "It said 'Mare for Sale – Name Your Price.' Sorry, Cal. It just caught my eye."

They had driven about another mile when suddenly Calvin pulled over and turned the Buick around. An old mare, he had thought. That just might be the perfect solution.

"What are you doing?" Ralph had asked.

Calvin, who was smiling with fresh enlightenment, turned to him. "We are going to see a man about a horse."

When they reached the sign, Calvin pulled the car over and got out. It was made out of ragged old barn wood, or so it appeared, and the lettering on it had been sloppily hand painted. He read it and re-read it before finally looking around to see the nearby property. A dirt road ran east right where the sign was posted, and there were no houses or other roads anywhere nearby.

"I'm guessing the seller can be found down this road, wouldn't you say Ralph?" Calvin asked.

Ralph shrugged. "I suppose, Cal. Sure would have been nice if they would have added an arrow or something."

Soon they were back in the car, following the dirt road. About a mile down and on the right, hidden by a group of trees, was a dilapidated white house, or at least, Calvin assumed it was white. Most of the paint had long since peeled off, and it didn't look like the owner much cared. The front porch was sagging in the middle, and an ancient screen door beat noisily against its frame, giving the place a haunted, empty feel.

Calvin had parked the car and shut it off, and soon they were both standing in the dirt drive looking around. They couldn't hear anything that sounded even close to human, so Cal began to holler.

"Hello! Hello! Is anyone home?"

The silence was the only sound, so he began to walk toward the rear of the place. Right then a voice came from behind them. Both men jumped at the unexpected sound.

"'Elp y'all?"

They turned to see a gray-haired old man wearing a tattered brown hat and equally tattered overalls. He had no teeth in his mouth, and he seemed to have not had a shave in that century. Calvin smiled at the sight; he was always amused by the locals and found the very look and sound of them warmed his heart.

"Yes sir," he replied. "Are you the gentleman with the old mare for sale?"

Sure enough, the old codger was. He led the two men out back to a broken down old barn that didn't look fit for a rat to live in. There they found an old horse. She was gray and white, and her mane was knotted and mangled. Her back slumped violently, forming a deep curve which made her look as though she had been ridden to the point of abuse. Calvin could also see that her feet hadn't been newly shod or received any treatment in a very long time, and she walked on her legs as if she were in horrible pain. He caught a quick glimpse of her broken brown teeth, and the sight made him cringe from disgust.

"'Er name's Maddie," the old man blurted out in his gravelly voice.

Cal approached the mare slowly, smiling, with his hand out, speaking her name in gentle soothing tones. "Maddie… what a good horse. What a pretty name for a pretty horse." He held his hand up to her nostrils; he could tell she was sniffing him by the movement of the nose alone. Otherwise, the rest of her head and body didn't move at all. "Good Maddie. That's a good girl."

While she familiarized herself with his scent, Calvin looked her over. Bugs were covering her face, but she could hardly exert the effort to shoo them away. Her right eye was a rich brown, but it was filled with exhaustion. There was hardly any zest or life left in the animal at all.

Her left eye was in bad shape. A milky cataract covered it, making Maddie's lack of sight very obvious. When she did attempt to look him over, she turned the right side of her head in his direction, and it broke his heart every time she did it. When the sign read 'old mare,' well, this old boy wasn't kidding.

"How old is she, sir?" he asked as he stroked her patchy hair.

"Name's Carter… Noah Carter," the old man stated gruffly as he approached Calvin and the mare. "I suppose I ain't never really been a sir. Hmmm, I reckon her to be right 'bout twenty-seven years. Yeah, that's about right, if it ain't damn close. She's been a tough old coot, too. Bet ya she's outlived most any other 'round these parts."

Calvin continued to look her over. "Why do you want to get rid of her? Is she sick? I mean, aside from all of the obvious issues I see."

Noah Carter shook his head. "Nope. Can't say Maddie has ever had any real sickness before. Nothing that she didn't get over quick, anyways. Nope. Just too old to take care of the old girl anymore myself, not the way she needs and deserves, and I ain't got the heart to put her down. Had 'er, 'er whole life. Born right 'ere she was."

Old man Noah kicked at a rock at his foot with the toe of his grubby, well-worn boot, and then continued in a low voice. "'Sides, I ain't got the money to give her what she needs. Just don't. She ain't gonna live forever; I just want her to be comfortable until her turn comes if you know what I mean."

Calvin nodded and threw a glance at Ralph, who looked about ready to cry. If Ralph was anything for sure, he was a true softy. But Calvin wasn't one to judge; he had an overabundance of compassion himself.

"That I understand, Mr. Carter," Calvin replied. "That I surely understand. So, how much were you looking to get for her?"

"I'm not sure, I guess." The man began to rub his beard with his palm, and he was staring hard at some invisible item on the ground. "I guess I was hoping for around fifty dollars, but now that I'm looking at her and seeing her a bit through your eyes, I realize that's not so reasonable."

Calvin began to scan his eyes around the place. He saw the broken down house; he was aware of the neglected property. He also keenly took note of the fact that the man before him looked to be about on his last leg himself. There was no scent of alcohol about him, so Cal knew the man was simply... old. None of this was because of vice; that was for sure.

"How about if I give you a hundred, Mr. Carter," he stated firmly. "You may as well not dicker with me, because that's my final offer."

The old man's eyes snapped up and met Calvin's, suddenly sparkling with new light. "Do ya mean it?" then, just as quickly as it came, the look disappeared from his face. "Whatcha gonna do with 'er?" His voice was filled with suspicion, and he almost spat the words from his mouth.

Calvin understood what the man was thinking immediately. "Oh, no! Please sir, don't misunderstand! I have a large stable; she would be the only horse and very comfortable. She would be very well cared for, and she would keep my wife and I company. Whatever she needs, she will have."

Noah Carter contemplated Calvin's words, shifting his eyes to the floor and beginning to rub his beard again. He remained still and thoughtful for quite some time, so Calvin and Ralph gave their attention to Maddie. It wouldn't do to appear overeager or pushy.

Finally, Mr. Carter spoke. "Whereabouts do ya live?"

Calvin proceeded to tell the man exactly where his property was, and it seemed that Carter was well aware of the place. Once he learned how close Maddie would be and was told that he was free to stop and see her any time he wanted, he was more than willing to shake on it and conduct the transaction. He even threw in Maddie's old, rickety horse trailer, so Calvin gave him an additional twenty dollars.

The Buick was equipped to tow smaller trailers and other items, and getting Maddie back home turned out to be a very easy task for the men. Soon, after another jaunt to town for supplies, Maddie was settled in, and her mood seemed to even perk up a bit. She filled her belly and lay directly down to rest, and she ended up sleeping that entire first night through.

It looked as though ancient old Maddie was going to be a part of the Cooper family, even if it wasn't for very long.

∞

Now, here it was, nearly a year later, and Calvin was sitting on his porch, rocking in the dark, recalling the day they brought Maddie home. He smiled at the memory, and he was happy she was with them. After all, if it weren't for Maddie, Calvin may have never discovered how far he had truly come in his work.

Yes, it was true: Calvin Cooper was a perfectionist. He could be fully aware that his formula was improving, and that it indeed was showing wonderful promise. But it wasn't right yet, and that fact made him frustrated with himself. It could work all day long, but that was only if the user engorged themselves with plate after plate all day long. He needed to make it smaller, easier to administer, and stronger, so fewer doses were needed for the highest level of effectiveness.

Maddie, after all, ate the mixture all day long...

He had spent the first month she was with him getting her into the best possible shape he could for the state she was in. First, he had a veterinarian come out and give her a head-to-hoof run down. She's in good health for a horse of her age, the man had said. Not sick, just old. Probably in pain.

He recommended that Cal put her down, but he explained he had made a promise, so the man had let the issue drop. Next, Calvin had her shoed, cleaned up, and groomed. He had her teeth taken care of by a professional, and then he not only researched her species extensively to learn all he could learn about proper diet and exercise, but he also had a professional breeder come, and he paid the man to help him. Soon, she was on a strict diet and exercise regimen that would ensure she would at least die healthy and happy.

By the time she was with the Coopers three months, she was almost a brand new horse, even though her age blared apparently. But she was happier, her eyes were brighter, and she moved a bit more easily. She also ate well and often, and she started to fatten up.

At that point, Calvin became convinced that it was time.

It was time for Maddie to begin a daily regimen of the formula.

For Maddie, administration of it was easy. For a human, it would take three or four excessively large doses, literally platefuls, daily just to stimulate minute constant change and maintain it. For a man or woman that would be next to impossible, not to mention exhausting, which is why Calvin continued to work on minimization and formula strength. But for Maddie, all he would have to do was add the formula, in the large doses, to her oats every day.

So, with Ralph by his side recording everything, Cal began. In the morning, he would put an entire days-worth in the mare's food. He actually raised the dosage due to her size, and he made sure it was thoroughly mixed into her oats.

At first, Maddie turned up her nose to it, and she actually stopped eating for three days. After the first day, Calvin realized she didn't like the flavor. It was then that he developed the Waba paste.

Waba was a tropical plant he had extracted derivatives from back in college. He found that the extract boosted the effectiveness of Silkex, only a small amount, but enough. The best part was that the sap from the Waba tasted fruity and sweet and was full of cleansing properties. So, with high hopes, Cal developed the Waba paste, and he blended that into Maddie's food as well.

Suddenly she began to eat like a horse, literally. He didn't have to sweet talk her in any way; she ate with gusto, and she loved it. Needless to say, Calvin was pleased. Now, all they had to do was keep watch and record changes.

After a week, he was sure he saw changes. Her mane seemed silkier, her coat seemed fuller, and she seemed to move more easily. But both Calvin and Ralph knew it was likely just high hopes, so they didn't let themselves get too excited.

Two weeks passed, then three. Finally, at the end of one month, the effects were undeniable: the formula was working, and working very well! It was actually more than Calvin could've dared to hope for.

At the end of thirty days, Maddie no longer had any bald patches in her coat; it was full and sleek. Her mane was much thicker, and the essential natural oils her body produced to keep it healthy had returned, as with her tail. She no longer crippled around; her movements were far more fluid. She had even been caught trying to prance a couple of times.

But the best part, the part that convinced both men, was the fact that the cataract on her eye was shrinking.

Calvin had not been allowing Elaina to visit Maddie, simply for the sake of study. Now he not only wanted her to see Maddie, but he also couldn't wait for it. He brought his wife out to the stable on the night of the thirtieth day.

He led Elaina out with a large handkerchief tied over her eyes. He didn't tell her what the surprise was, he simply told her to brace herself. She giggled the entire way, and it tickled him.

"Okay, Elaina," he said as he positioned her before Maddie's quarters. The horse stood before them, still and waiting, as if she knew what was going on and wanted to see the look on his wife's face. "Are you ready?"

"Yes, yes! Quit being silly now!"

Calvin removed the blind and watched her closely. This would be the true test, the real measure of how far the formula had brought the old mare. Elaina hadn't seen her, so if the change were as drastic as he thought, it would be obvious.

Her mouth immediately dropped open, and her eyes widened. The smile left her face, and she appeared to be in a state of mild shock. Calvin couldn't help but smile as he waited for her to speak.

"Cal, is this... is this Maddie?"

He crossed his arms over his chest and glanced at Ralph, who was writing vigorously in his notebook. "Yep."

She began to walk back and forth before the horse, looking at her body in the light, taking in all she could see. Maddie watched her and appeared to be amused, as crazy as it seemed. After a long bit, Elaina stopped pacing and began to shake her head.

"You did this?" she asked.

Calvin nodded. "What do you think?"

"You... you can hardly tell it's even her, Cal! She looks ten years younger, maybe more!"

He did not respond, he only watched her expressions. "I don't even know what to say. Does this mean you have it? The formula is right? And the dosage?"

"Well," he began. "The formula is correct, and I suppose the dosage, yes. But the problem is that the amount of administration is so large, and on a daily basis, it is not at all practical. Maddie made it easy; after all, she is a horse."

They were silent once again, then he said, "I want you and me to take it, Elaina."

She turned to him quickly, a very serious look on her face. "No, Calvin."

"Why? What do you mean? You want to wait until I have the dose perfected? A pill, perhaps?"

Elaina shook her head. "Just no, Cal. No."

With that Elaina turned and walked back to the house without another word. Calvin looked at Ralph, confused, and Ralph returned the look. "I'll be right back, okay?"

He caught up with his wife just as she was reaching the front door. "Elaina, what's wrong? Don't you know I would never give you anything that would hurt you?"

Calvin followed her into the living room, where she sat in her rocker and picked up her crocheting. "It's not that, love. I just… No."

Having been married to the woman for forty years, he could tell by her tone alone that she was serious. Well, he thought, no need to push her now. It is likely the amount she would be eating; she was always watching her weight.

"Fine, dear," he said calmly as he bent down and kissed her cheek. "I'll let it go. I'll be back in as soon as Ralph, and I finish up outside."

On the way to the barn, he turned it over in his mind. Maybe she was concerned that it was dangerous for a human. Yes, that was it! She didn't understand that there was not one unnatural thing in there, nothing that could ever hurt, only help. Now he had only two things to work on: making it smaller and less demanding to take and finding a way to show her that it was safe for human beings.

∞

Now, almost a year later, he sat rocking in the darkness, thinking and thinking. Yes, he was still struggling with the administration, but he was more concerned with a human trial. If he experimented on himself and she found out, and she certainly would, oh, he didn't even want to think about it.

Ralph was not an option, either. It was simply not okay to test on someone in good health, with no foreseen issues, not to mention he was family at this point. No, there had to be another way.

He pushed the issue from his mind for the thousandth time.

The fact was, now, months later, Maddie was like a young mare again. She galloped and ran, her sight was perfect, and she was gorgeous to look at. Yes, he was so close he could nearly taste it.

Tomorrow, he would visit Noah Carter and see if he would like to visit his Maddie. He hadn't contacted them or been around since the second month she was with them. Calvin had been to see him a few times, but the old man had been far too tired to leave home. To be honest, Cal had wondered if he had cancer or something. Heck, he didn't even know if old Carter was alive. He would go see him first thing in the morning, and he would take Maddie with him.

R.W.K. Clark

CHAPTER 7

First thing the next morning, Calvin and Ralph had Elaina pack a couple of lunches, including an extra for Noah Carter. Next, they groomed Maddie, filled her feedbag with plenty of oats and formula, and packed her up in the brand new horse trailer Calvin had purchased for her a couple of months back. It didn't take very long to get going at all, and soon they were on the road taking the short drive to Carter's place.

When they pulled up, the house and property were deathly quiet. Calvin told Ralph to stay put, and he went up to the house through the rear entrance. He learned during his last visit that the front porch wasn't safe to use, and nearly broke his ankle in the lesson.

"Mr. Carter?" He yelled after he gave the back door a few good bangs. "It's Calvin Cooper. Mr. Carter, are you home, sir?"

He waited in silence for a moment and looked around the place. It had become so overgrown and broken down that he had a hard time believing anyone would stay, even the gruff old man. When he didn't get a response, he gave the door a few more hard bangs.

"Mr. Carter!"

Suddenly, he could hear what sounded like uneven footsteps from inside, then, "I'ma comin' dammit! Give an old man time, would ya?"

Calvin smiled and motioned for Ralph to get out of the truck and join him. His assistant just reached him as the back door flew open. There stood Noah Carter, giving them both the evil eye.

He looked like death warmed over. Any bit of fat he had on his body was completely gone. The only reason his pants stayed up was that they were overalls, but they bagged on his skinny body terribly. His skin was slightly yellowed, and his hair was thin to the point of falling out.

"Ah, yeah! Cooper! Nearly forgot 'bout ya!" Carter tried to smile, but it seemed that even that much effort drained him. "How's my girl Maddie?"

"Well, that's sort of why we came," Cal replied. "You look tired, Noah. Do you want to visit inside?"

The old man shook his head and made his way through the door on shaking legs. He let it slam behind him and then took a seat on a broken-down bench next to it which was surrounded by weeds. He closed his eyes in pain and gave a grunt as he sat.

"Nah, more work for me in the end," he said. "Something happen to old Maddie, did it? Lord finally take 'er?"

Calvin glanced at Ralph and shook his head. "No, nothing like that. Are you ill, Noah?"

"I'ma dyin', can't ya see that?"

Neither man said anything in response at first, then

Ralph said, "What is it, sir?"

Carter adjusted himself on the hard bench, trying to find what comfort he could. "I dunno. Lotta pain in my side, skin getting all pasty and yella. Tired all the time. Old and dying."

Calvin asked, "You haven't seen a doctor?"

"Butchers they are!" the man grumbled. "And damn costly ones at that. I have a daughter in Spokane. She left home to go to college way back. She came to check on me a month ago and tried to get me to town, but nah. Finally, she let me be about it. I'll die right here, thank you very much."

There was a brief lull in the conversation. Neither Calvin nor Ralph knew quite what to say next, and it was finally Carter who broke the silence. "So, what's this about Maddie?"

Calvin's eyes lit up immediately, glad for the change of subject. "Can I sit next to you, Noah?"

The old man nodded toward the empty space, then said to Ralph, "Go ahead and pull up that crate there. It'll hold ya."

Ralph obliged as Calvin sat. "I think I told you before that I'm a scientist."

Noah nodded.

"Well, my work involves making people look and feel younger," he began. "I actually sold a formula that got rid of wrinkles when I was in college. But for the last forty years or so, I have been trying to find a more… permanent solution. One that not only makes people look younger but restores their health and makes them feel younger too."

Carter burst out laughing, but the laughter gave way to a terrible cough that wracked his entire body. For a moment Cal and Ralph thought they might lose him on the spot, but after a bit, the cough began to subside, and within a couple of minutes, the old man got control. He spat on the ground and turned to Calvin.

"That's the funniest thing I ever heard."

Calvin smiled at him. "I'm sure. Well, Maddie was so old and sick, and she was dying, you know."

"Ayuh."

"So," he continued slowly, "I began to give her my treatment. It's completely natural so it could do no harm, and I figured she had nothing to lose."

Now Carter was just staring at him through yellowing eyes.

"It seemed to work, Noah." With that, Calvin nodded at Ralph, who jumped up and headed around the house for the trailer.

Noah knit his brow. "What do ya mean, it seemed to work?"

"I think it would be better to show you; I don't think you would believe me if I explained it."

Ralph came around the corner then, leading Maddie by her rein. Carter had his back to them, and he was still giving Cal the evil eye. Once they returned, Cal put his hand on the old man's shoulder and smiled.

"Look, Noah."

The old man struggled to turn his body in the direction which Calvin had nodded. Cal stood up and moved around so he could see the reaction on Noah's face. It was something he wouldn't miss for the world; it was the very reason for his work.

Once he repositioned, Carter lifted his head.

"Oh, my… my, my," he whispered, his eyes wide with disbelief. "That's my Maddie."

"Yes, sir. It is."

Calvin had expected that he would have to convince the man, but he could tell right away that it would not be needed. Carter knew that horse right away, and Maddie knew him. She began to snort and whinny and stomp with joy, and once again it appeared she was smiling.

Noah tried to rise, but he only made it up a few inches before sitting right down again. Calvin rushed to him. No one needed this man to hurt himself at a time like this.

"Ralph, bring her to him."

As soon as the horse reached Noah Carter, she buried her nose in his neck. His skinny arms wrapped around her head, and he began to hug her as though she were a long lost friend. Tears began to fall down the cheeks of all three of those grown men.

"Oh, Maddie, Maddie!" Carter exclaimed. "Look at you, girlie! Just look!"

She lifted her head and let out a loud whinny that Calvin was sure could be heard for miles. Then she broke away and ran twice around the dirt yard before returning and burying her head in his neck once again.

Cal and Ralph let the two alone, watching and

feeling the joy of the moment. It was beautiful. Calvin had done more than restore her youth; he had given these two another moment in time.

After about ten minutes, Maddie plopped right down on the ground next to the old man. Carter fished a filthy handkerchief from the breast pocket of his overalls. He wiped his eyes and blew his nose loudly. Then he turned to the men.

"What did you do, Cooper?" he asked. "What's the trick?"

Calvin shrugged, smiling through his own tears. "No trick, Mr. Carter. I have been working on this for the majority of my life. I don't have it perfected yet. I mean, the amount that has to be taken daily needs to be lessened. In other words, I need to increase the strength. But I think it's working."

Carter looked at his horse, who had pretty much laid her head in his lap. "Yep. I'd say it's working."

He petted and kissed Maddie's head again, speaking in low loving tones words that were just between the two of them. After a bit, he looked back at Calvin. His face was serious, but his yellow eyes were clear.

"My daughter left under bad terms all them years ago," he began. "Didn't want her to leave, didn't want her to go to no damn college. Wanted her to stay here where I could keep her safe and sound. She was all I had left of her mother, ya see."

He sat back hard against the back of the bench. With one hand he continued to stroke Maddie's head, but he ran the other through his thin hair and shook his head. "But she wouldn't have it. She had a 'scholarship,' and she was of age; she could do what she wanted. The day she left we fought so bad I was sure I would never see her again. I didn't, not 'til she came last time, and we ended up fighting again." The old man smiled bitterly at the memory. "This time it was because I wouldn't do what she wanted, and I made it a point to rub that fact in her face. Humph."

Calvin and Ralph remained silent, listening respectfully to the story the man was trying to get off his chest.

"I love her so, my daughter Ruth," he said. "More than you could know. Do you have kids?"

Both men shook their heads.

"Well, what have ya. I would do just about anything to make it right before I die." Carter looked down at Maddie again, then asked in a sure, strong voice. "Will ya do it? Will ya give it to me and make me young again? Just long enough to make it right?"

Calvin looked at Ralph in surprise before walking to the crate and sitting down. He leaned toward Carter with his elbows on his knees and thought for a moment before responding. The question had caught him off guard.

"Mr. Carter," he began. "I'm sorry to hear about your relationship with Ruth. I cannot pretend to imagine how that must feel." He paused a moment. "But you need to understand, this has never been used on humans. I haven't perfected the strength or the dosage."

"But you said it's natural."

Calvin stood and began his pacing. "Yes, yes it is, it's all natural, every last ingredient in it. But I don't know how it will respond to the human body, or how much it will take, or anything for that matter."

"No better way to learn than to use it on a person, wouldn't ya say?"

Calvin stopped pacing and looked at the old man, then Ralph. Carter had a point. If he went through the proper channels, it would be years before the FDA allowed human consumption, if even during his lifetime.

"'Sides," Carter continued as he smiled at Maddie and stroked her. "I'm nearin' ninety. I'ma dyin', of that much I'm sure. I got nothin' to lose, do you?"

Calvin took a deep breath. "I'll tell you what, Noah. Let me discuss this with Ralph... he's my assistant. I need to get his thoughts. I also need to talk to my wife. You see, I had some issues with the law over testing on rats, and if you decide to..."

"I ain't gonna decide no such thing!" Carter hollered his response as loud as he could, and there was both impatience and anger in his voice. "If I take it and it hurts me, I die. If I don't, I die. But if I take it and it helps, well, then you learn more, and I get to be stronger and healthier, am I right?"

Cal looked to Ralph, who shrugged. "Look, Noah. I'm willing, I guess. I see your point. But I have to talk to my wife. You understand."

The old man nodded. "Fine. Talk to her. When will I know?"

"I'll talk to her today when I get home," Calvin said. "If she agrees, and that's a big 'if,' Ralph and I will sit down and plan a regimen for you. I will come back and let you know tomorrow."

"Deal."

"But!" Calvin exclaimed. "The only way and I mean the only way I will do this is if you agree to come to my lab for the duration of the initial stages of the treatment."

"Now look…" Carter began.

"Noah, the only way! I need to have you there so I can be safe in all aspects," he said. "You will have good meals and a comfortable bed and warm place to sleep. It's the only way, and I mean it."

The old man thought for less than a minute. "Fine. I'll do it your way."

With that, Calvin and Ralph let Maddie and Noah have some more time together. He had wanted to keep her, but Cal explained her diet was her treatment, and he had brought no extra food. After about a half-hour, the two men and the horse packed things up and headed for home. Now, it was time to talk to Elaina.

R.W.K. Clark

CHAPTER 8

Calvin and Elaina sat on the porch swing staring at the wide-open, clear Montana sky. He held her close to him, reveling in the scent of her hair and the feel of her body. How thankful he was to have this woman for his wife.

They had been married more than forty years, and he loved her more now than the day they first met. She was smart, funny, and beautiful, but more than anything, she kept him grounded. As a scientist, he could get off into left field at times, so this was one of her most valuable characteristics, in his opinion.

"You know I love you?" he asked her.

"Mmm," she replied. "You know I do, love."

He thought for a moment. He wanted to ask her some important things, but he didn't want to spoil the mood by asking them the wrong way. Today had been amazing; she agreed to allow Calvin to bring Carter and treat him with the formula, and it didn't take much convincing. She had the same outlook as the old man: what did he have to lose at this point? Her only requirement was that he sleep and live in the house so she could care for him. Her 'office' was empty, so she made Ralph and Calvin go to Randalia and purchase a bed for him, and then she had spent the afternoon finishing the room for his arrival.

∞

Ralph had prepared a new file for the man and got all of the lab necessities ready. Calvin whipped up a big batch of the Waba paste, and for the first time, he actually got a taste of it when, in haste, he licked it off his finger. No wonder Maddie loved it! It was wonderful. It had a pleasing texture, similar to apple butter, but it tasted like a cross between grapes and pomegranates. Calvin loved it, and he decided right then and there that he would eat it himself with his food. He thought it would make an amazing sandwich.

∞

"Thank you for your support, Elaina," he said as he stroked her arm. "I don't know what I will ever do if I lose you."

She patted his leg lovingly. "You will go on. You know that."

"I couldn't bear it."

"You could, and you would," she replied.

"Elaina," he said slowly, "Why will you not allow me to treat you? Do you not trust me? Do you think I will hurt you?"

She sat up and looked at him. "Oh, Calvin, no! Never! Love, I really can't explain it, only to say that I am happy being me, just the way I am, just the age I am. Do you understand?"

"But you could feel twenty again."

Elaina sighed. "Look, do you find me old and unattractive?"

"No, dear," he replied. "Never."

"Well, I'm content. Listen, I have considered it before," she said. "It just isn't for me, but if I ever change my mind, I will come to you right away."

Calvin smiled at her. "Promise?"

"Promise."

He leaned forward and pressed his lips gently against hers. She responded right away, and the feel of her kiss began to cause a stirring he hadn't felt in a very long time. Suddenly, as they kissed, he realized he had neglected her terribly, and at that moment he wanted to make it up to her.

"I love you more than life," he whispered against her mouth.

"And I you..."

They made love that night for the first time in months, and Calvin felt himself falling harder and harder in love with her with each passing second. When they were finished, and Elaina lay sleeping in his arms, her soft breath on his cheek, he knew he could not lose her. He would convince her, somehow. He would convince her to live forever with him.

No matter what it took.

∞

The men arrived back at the house with Noah Carter shortly after ten o'clock the following morning. Noah had been a simple relocation: he brought only a single change of clothing with him consisting of underwear, socks, a stained and torn t-shirt, and a pair of holey overalls which Calvin doubted were clean. When Elaina saw the items, she put them in the washer right away, and then abruptly left for town in the Buick to purchase some clothing and personal items for the old man.

The first thing they did, after showing him his room, of course, was take him out to the lab to weigh him in and get his medical history. The man stood five-foot-nine-inches, but he weighed only one-hundred-three pounds.

"That will change," Calvin told him with a smile. "That was one of the first things to change with Maddie."

Next, they got as much of a medical history from the man as they could, but it wasn't much. None of his family had been fans of the medical profession, but all of them had lived well into their nineties. In both Calvin and Ralph's opinion, this was a good sign.

Next, they served him up a plateful of the formula, mixed well with Waba paste. The portion was tailored to his weight, but it was really more of a guess than anything. Thankfully they had worked with rats and Maddie, so it was something of an educated guess, at least.

"What the 'ell is this?" Noah asked a look of distaste on his face.

Calvin smiled, amused by the old man's reaction. "That, sir, is the treatment, and you will be eating it three times a day. I told you, I am still working on making it stronger, with smaller, less frequent dosages."

"I should hope so. Good Lord."

Calvin knew it was not appetizing in appearance, and that was also something he had been focusing on, but for the time being, this was what he had. He and Ralph sat down to eat with the man; Elaina had made a peanut butter and jelly sandwich for Ralph, and Calvin had a sandwich of fruit remains and Waba paste which he had prepared for himself. It certainly made the waste go down easier, anyway.

Carter's first bite changed his mind about the food entirely. "Hey!" he said. "That's not so bad... not so bad a'tall! I could do without the mushy fruits and stuff, but whatever that jelly is, it's tasty Calvin!"

"That's my own special recipe," Calvin replied. "I made it so Maddie would eat the formula because she hated it. Turns out the stuff was so good I eat it myself, see?" He opened his sandwich and showed it to Noah. "Well, I figure if my formula falls through, I can always market Waba paste, as I call it."

The men continued their meal, and when Ralph was done, he began recording the details of it in Noah's chart. When the man had finally cleaned his plate, Calvin took him to the house and settled him in so he could get a nap. That was pretty much all old man Carter did for his first week with them. It wasn't until his fifth or sixth night that he started coming out of his room more often. Calvin would find him in the kitchen visiting with Elaina, or in the living room under a blanket, watching a television program with her. To him, these things were wonderful signs, and he made sure they were all recorded.

On his seventh day, Carter was taken back out to the lab where he was weighed and given the once-over. Calvin did a complete head-to-toe, which he would do once a week for the duration of his stay. He wanted to be sure there were no negative changes, either in health or appearance, when it came to the man's body.

"Well, Mr. Carter, you currently weigh one-hundred-eleven pounds," Calvin said to him as he helped him off the scale. "That's an eight-pound gain, you know."

"Eight?" Carter asked with disbelief. "What the heck is in that stuff yer feedin' me?"

Calvin chuckled. "It's all natural, and it's good for you," he replied. "How are you feeling?" He put his stethoscope up to the man's chest and waited for an answer.

"Ya know, I have to say, I feel okay." He cleared his throat and continued. "I'm still tired, but the fact is, I don't even remember the last time I had a fit of the coughs. I was havin' 'em ev'ry day, ya know."

Cal held up a tongue depressor, and the man opened wide. His tongue had been coated when he first arrived; it still was, but it appeared to be much thinner and not so white. His throat looked fine.

"Less coughing," Calvin stated with a nod to Ralph, who was writing furiously in Carter's file. Next, he took his penlight and prepared to shine it in Noah's eyes. "Just try to look straight ahead, okay?"

The man obeyed. The first thing Cal noticed wasn't his pupils or the way they dilated. Rather, he noticed that the yellow was fading. No, not just fading; his whites were almost normal.

Now he stepped back, and after adjusting the overhead lighting, took a good look at the overall man. Yes, it was true. Even the yellow in his skin was fading; it was obvious.

"Mr. Carter, as you know, I am not a doctor, but I would like to draw some blood," Calvin said. "I suspect you have been in the throes of liver failure, and I would like to get a blood count to be sure. Also, it will help me monitor your blood sugar, as well as make sure your body is handling the formula properly, okay?"

Carter said nothing, only held his arm out for Carter to prick with his needle.

As he drew the man's blood, he thought about the progress. Yes, he was encouraged. He had to admit, he could hardly wait to see how things went the following week.

But he wouldn't have to wait long to find out.

∞

The following week was a busy one for Calvin and Ralph. They were spending double-time in the laboratory working on the potency of the formula, hoping to downsize the dosage and frequency. Cal didn't want to use the new dosage on Mr. Carter, so on Monday, he and Ralph drove to Randalia. There, they would pick up five rats, and they would also get some new supplies for the lab itself. During the drive, they discussed how excited they both were to see Noah Carter's progress on his weekly check, which came on Friday.

Calvin had not seen much of the man since his last check, except for in passing. He spent a lot of time in his room resting or reading, according to Elaina, but she told them he ate well and always cleaned his plate. They had upped his dosage a bit due to his slight weight gain, but she said he polished it off every time. They were happy and encouraged.

In Randalia they got their errands done fairly quickly, as well as the grocery shopping Calvin needed to do in order to replenish his food supply. It wouldn't do to run out of ingredients for the formula, especially since they had their patient and were working so hard to improve the product. It was a long day, and by the time they pulled out of the market parking lot, they were both looking forward to getting back home.

As they neared the edge of town, there was a massive 'bang!' from behind the car, and the vehicle began to swerve violently to and fro. Calvin maintained control and got the car to the side of the road, where the two men got out to see what had happened.

It was a flat, and not just any flat. The rim of the tire was badly damaged due to the speed at which they had been traveling. "Well," Cal said, "looks like we had better hike back to that mechanic I saw a couple blocks up."

So they did. But when they got there, they were informed by the man that he didn't deal in either tires or rims. His brother had a tire shop in Twixt, so the man called him. He agreed to bring both items, but he couldn't do it until the following day, as his wife and mother-in-law had his truck and were doing some shopping in Butte and wouldn't be back until late.

So, the man from the shop towed the Buick. Calvin and Ralph took the groceries from the car and made sure it was secured, then they walked six more blocks into town, where they rented a single room in a small hotel. The manager was a nice old lady who let them store their groceries in the freezer of her apartment in the back. Once they got settled in, Calvin telephoned Elaina to let her know what had happened.

"Hello, dear," he began. "Ralph and I blew a tire, and it can't be fixed until tomorrow."

"Are you okay?" she asked.

Cal sighed. "Yes, we're both fine. Got the groceries in the manager's fridge here, and we have a room, but we won't be back until around noon tomorrow. I hope you are going to be okay."

"I'll be fine," she replied. "Calvin, Mr. Carter came out of his room for a while today. As a matter of fact, he is still out."

Calvin knit his brow. "Is he okay?"

"Yes, yes. I think so," she said. "Oh, I wish you were coming home. I think you need to see him for yourself."

"Elaina, what's wrong? Is he ill?"

She was silent for a moment. Finally, she said, "No, I don't think so, but I'm not going to talk about it when

I don't know for sure. I'll take care of things, and I'll call if there are any problems, but you need to come home as soon as possible."

"Elaina…" Calvin heard a voice in the background.

"Yes, Mr. Carter," he heard his wife say. "Look, Cal, I have to go. Mr. Carter needs me. Please get home. I love you."

Just like that, the call was disconnected.

Calvin was worried right away. "Ralph, Elaina says something is going on with Noah, but she won't give me any details. What do you think it is?"

"I don't know," Ralph replied. "Did she say he is sick?"

Cal shrugged. "She didn't say anything. Well, I suppose all we can do is get through the night and get back as soon as possible."

CHAPTER 9

Neither Calvin nor Ralph got very much sleep that night. Both stayed up discussing Noah Carter, staring into the darkness, anxiety coursing through their bodies. Calvin had called Elaina one more time to give her the number to the hotel in case she needed to get ahold of him. He also tried to get more information out of her, but she held her water. Finally, he came to the conclusion that if Noah had experienced a setback, or was ill, she would let him know. He needed to trust her and let it go.

By the time they had checked out of their room, got their groceries from the manager, and walked the short distance to the mechanic's shop, the Buick was ready and waiting for them. Calvin was so relieved that he gave the man an extra twenty dollars, and before he knew it, they were back on the road home. It took all the strength he had inside of him to keep the car at a reasonable, safe speed during the drive.

Finally, they were there, and Calvin asked Ralph to take the groceries to the lab, unpack them, and meet him in the house. The men separated, and Calvin jogged to the front door. He wanted to get the issue dealt with as soon as possible, whatever it was.

"Elaina? I'm home, dear!" Calvin threw the door open and shouted the words before he was even inside. "Elaina!"

"I'm right here, Calvin," she said in a hurried voice as she walked quickly from the kitchen.

Cal sighed. "What is going on? Where is Noah? Is he okay?"

Elaina took her husband by the arm. "Calvin, calm down and have a seat." She led him to the dining room and pulled out his chair at the head of the table. "I told you, he isn't sick. He's just... different. Had he been sick, I would have told you. Now calm yourself."

The sternness in her voice got his attention, and Calvin closed his mouth abruptly. Elaina disappeared into the kitchen, returning with a steaming cup of coffee, which she placed before him. She then patted him on the shoulder and planted a lingering kiss on his cheek.

"Where is Ralph?" she asked.

Calvin took a drink of the delicious black liquid, then set the cup down gently. "He will be in shortly. The groceries needed to be put away as soon as possible."

Right then the assistant came into the room. "So, what's going on? Is Noah okay?"

"Yes, Ralph," Elaina replied. "He's in the bathroom. Sit down; I'll get you some coffee, and then I'll fetch him."

Soon, both men were drinking coffee and waiting

anxiously for Elaina to return with Noah. What could be the issue that they needed to see the man, as she had said? Calvin felt irritated, to say the least.

"If he isn't sick, she shouldn't have mentioned it at all," he said gruffly to Ralph. "I'm going to have a word with her about judgment. I have never been so worried in my life."

At that moment, Elaina came around the corner with Noah Carter. Calvin looked up at them, startled. When Ralph noticed, he turned around to look as well, and immediately dropped his coffee cup. It shattered all over the table.

Noah Carter looked like a forty-year-old man.

His posture was straight and strong. His weight was completely proportionate to his height. The man had shaved his scraggly beard, and fresh, healthy pink skin covered his face. His eyes were clear and bright, and his hair was thick and black. He was smiling.

"Who is this?" Calvin asked; he was genuinely confused.

The man chuckled, and Elaina said, "You don't recognize your own patient?"

Calvin stood up, his eyes glued to the man before him. He walked toward him as if in a trance, and when he reached him, he couldn't help but touch the man's face and hair. This had to be a joke; it couldn't be real. But he knew in his heart Elaina would never pull such a prank.

"Ralph, get his file."

Ralph jumped up from the table and left running.

Calvin began to walk around the man, who now appeared to be ten years younger than he. He was wearing denim dungarees and a button-down plaid shirt, both of which he assumed Elaina had purchased for him when he first came. They fit him perfectly.

When he got back to face the man, he said, "Noah?"

The man smiled broadly. "Yes, Calvin. It's me."

His voice was strong, with no rasp or gruffness to it at all. Calvin even took notice of the fact that he seemed to have every tooth in his mouth, and he could not explain it. He wasn't even sure what to say or where to begin.

"How did this take place? Overnight? Slowly? Sit down; we need to talk."

Ralph appeared with his file and a pen. He sat in the same spot, and Elaina began to clear the broken china from the table and clean up the coffee so he could work. Noah took a seat as well, smiling at Ralph, who was staring at him, dumbfounded.

"Well," Noah began. "I began to notice that I felt better the second day I was here, and I felt a bit better each day. But I have to admit, I hadn't spent much time in the mirror. It seemed I was so busy sleeping."

He paused, then continued. "I had been staying in my room reading because I didn't want to bother anyone. Elaina brought my food on a tray, and she would knock to let me know it was there; she was so polite! Anyway, I would eat it and bring the tray out to the kitchen, but no one was ever here.

"Yesterday morning, I got up and filled the bath. I

got cleaned up and was drying off in my room when I realized I had left my hairbrush in your bathroom," he said. "I dressed and went to get it, and while I was in there, I ran it through my hair. I guess out of habit I looked in the mirror. I… I couldn't believe my eyes, Calvin. I mean, look at me!"

No one said a word in response. Ralph was so busy writing that Cal had a hard time believing he heard a word. "Are you listening, Ralph?"

"To everything!"

Noah continued. "I was so shocked that I came out to find Elaina, but she wasn't in the house. At first, I was going to wait in here for her, but I was too excited. I found her in the garden. She - ."

"I was in the garden," Elaina cut in excitedly. "I saw him come out the front door, so I assumed he was a burglar, and I got all frightened. I said, 'Who are you? What do you want?'"

Noah picked up the story once again. "I told her, 'It's me, Noah.' I tell you two, it took me an hour to convince her!" With that, both he and Elaina burst out laughing at the memory, and all Calvin could do was look at Ralph, stunned.

Finally, he spoke. "This was very fast. I didn't expect this at all." He stood and began pacing. "We need to get you out to the lab and give you a check-up. You are still taking your formula, yes? Eating your meals?"

Noah nodded enthusiastically.

"Okay, then," Cal said. "Out we go, men. Elaina, we will be back when we are finished."

With that, the three men left the house, leaving Elaina standing with a broad smile on her face. Oh, she was so proud of her husband. He was an extraordinary man, and he was accomplishing everything he set out to do. She could never want more out of life than she had.

Suddenly, a flash of heat and nausea came over her. The room began to spin, and she had to grab the back of a chair to steady herself. She stood, shaking severely, for several moments. At last it passed, but she was drenched in sweat, and there were stars before her eyes.

That was when she realized her nose was bleeding.

She grabbed a tissue from the box on the table and held it to her nose. There she stood, her eyes toward the sky, putting pressure on her nose and fighting the lightheadedness which threatened to floor her. She could feel the tissue soaking up the blood.

Elaina struggled a bit and sat down at the table until she felt normal again. After about three tissues the nosebleed stopped, and soon she was stable. It was quite unnerving, to say the least.

That was the first time that ever happened, and she assumed she needed to eat something. She made her way into the kitchen and prepared an early lunch for herself. She would be fine; she simply needed to watch her excitement level.

She kept the incident to herself, never telling Calvin about it at all.

∞

For the next month, Calvin and Ralph kept a close eye on Noah Carter. Calvin was concerned about maintenance. If they gave him too much formula or continued to give it to him, would he continually get younger? If they cut him off or tapered it, would he revert to his old self?

These were all new questions for the two men. Maddie simply ate her daily portions, and she seemed to be just fine, neither aging nor getting younger. All Calvin could assume was that her dosage was perfect for her.

But humans were not horses, and Calvin had not expected such success with Noah. So, in an effort to figure out things as quickly as they possibly could, they began doing daily checkups as opposed to weekly ones. At first, things were a bit sketchy: if they cut back on his dose, he would be tired and moody the following day, even looking pale. If they raised it too much, he would decrease in age by two or three years overnight. It was very touch and go for quite some time.

By the second month after the major change, Calvin had come much closer to figuring out Noah's dosage. It needed a bit of tweaking here and there, but he was getting close. By month three, he added an exercise regimen to the dose he was giving the man, and things stabilized perfectly.

∞

One evening, Noah approached Calvin and Elaina as they sat on the porch in the swing.

"Elaina, do you mind if I have a word with your husband, please?"

She jumped right up. "Of course, Noah! Calvin, I'll

see you in the house, love."

When she was out of sight and earshot, Calvin motioned for Noah to sit next to him. "What can I help you with?"

"I want to leave; I want to travel to be with my daughter."

Calvin sat in stunned silence, not sure what to say. The revelation was very abrupt, and he didn't quite know how to deal with it. For one thing, his daughter Ruth had no idea what her father had been up to. For another, Calvin didn't know how to go about proceeding with the treatment if Noah left. Sure, he could send a certain amount of formula with the man, but it would eventually run out. Then what?

"Noah, if you leave I cannot guarantee this will last," he finally said. "I cannot treat you from here if you are in Spokane. I cannot monitor you. Eventually, without formula, you would most certainly revert."

The man nodded and looked into the sky. "I have thought about that, Calvin," he replied. "I am very, very appreciative of what you have done for me, I want you to know that. But I never wanted to live forever. I only wanted to live long enough to make things right with Ruth, and I can do that now."

Calvin could tell that Noah had thought things through. He had probably had this in mind all along, from the way it sounded. Oddly enough, he understood the man's way of thinking.

"I can send you with about a week's worth of the formula; you will have to add it to your food," he stated finally. He turned to Noah. "Will you call? Will you keep me posted on your welfare?"

Noah clasped him on the arm affectionately. "You have given me a priceless gift, my friend. That is the very least I can do. I have no money to offer you, Cal."

"I don't want your money," Cal said. "I want you to be happy."

∞

The very next day, Calvin telephoned Noah Carter's daughter, and after he explained who he was, he told her that her father wanted to be with her, that he wanted to talk with her. Then, he and Elaina left Noah alone with the phone. He would have to do the convincing.

Ruth came to pick up her father three days later, and she was dumbfounded at what she found. Noah had to prove who he was through the relation of memories and a couple of worn photos he carried in his tattered leather wallet. Those wouldn't have been necessary, though; she remembered the wallet above everything else. Together they left, and Ruth took her father home to Spokane, where they would get to know each other again after so many years.

∞

Six months later, Ruth Carter Wells called the Coopers to inform them that her father had passed away. It turned out that he had slowly, but surely, gotten older, and after four months, his previous sickness had returned with a vengeance. It ravaged him mercifully quickly. She thanked them for all they had done.

But Calvin Cooper heard none of that. He heard nothing of the thanks or the wonderful blessing of reconciliation. He heard no words about how quickly he had gone and had been in no pain. All he heard was that his formula had failed. He became dreadfully determined.

Somehow, he would make it last…

CHAPTER 10

1990

The situation with Noah Carter, and the intense obsessive work which followed exhausted Calvin to the point of near collapse. He had hit a massive brick wall regarding the formula; he couldn't seem to hit the nail on the head as far as concentrating it, nor could he seem to figure out how to strengthen or minimize the dosage. It seemed that anyone who would use it would have to forego the enjoyment of all regular food just to be able to eat three platefuls of it a day. It was too filling and too weak.

All of this took such a toll on Elaina that she became very upset, even losing weight and becoming a bit withdrawn. Finally, she requested, quite firmly, that he had to take a vacation with her; they needed to get away together. After all, she had said, they had never taken a vacation together in all the years they had been married. So, they decided that on their forty-fifth anniversary, they would travel to Switzerland, a place she had always dreamed of going.

Calvin knew that his work, and the time he spent on it, was wearing his wonderful wife very thin indeed. She hadn't told him this outright aside from wanting a vacation, but he could tell just by looking at her. The bags under her eyes and the slowness of her step wore heavy on his heart. How could he continue to do this to her? He had to give in somewhere, had to think of her first at some point. So taking her to Switzerland was the very least he could do.

After all, Elaina never complained, never nagged. The times when he did suggest giving up, she would get angry, telling him that he had invested his entire life to this, and he had come way too far to quit. She wouldn't hear of it. Calvin loved her so much. If only she knew how he sat up at night gazing at her sleeping face. If only she were aware of how often he found himself daydreaming of her soft skin and singsong voice while he was working, then she would know of his great love.

He would perfect the formula; he would make it right and convince her to take it with him. Then, after all the years he had neglected her, he could devote his time to her and her alone, and he would most certainly do that indeed. She deserved it. Never, in the history of the world, had a man been married to a softer, more loving, or more generous woman than his Elaina.

But there was something she had been keeping from him, something she knew would distract him and take his mind from his dream. Her dizzy spells had increased. It was not as if she had them daily; actually, she had only experienced them about ten times since the first one, back when Noah Carter's youth had become obvious. She was concerned about them, but she had herself convinced it was simply her body responding to its age. If she were to go see their doctor, Dr. Hal Bergstrom in Twixt, Calvin would know, and he would not be able to focus, and therefore, he would never accomplish what he had set out to do so many years ago.

No, she would simply take it easy. She would eat right and take a nice walk every day. She moved slowly about the house when she did her daily chores, and she kept a smile on her face whenever Calvin or Ralph was near. As far as yard work, she continued to take care of her flower garden, but she hired a young man from Twixt, a junior high school boy, to mow their lawn once a week in the summer and shovel for them when needed during the winter months. Calvin had no problem with this; she needed to be spoiled, and he enjoyed doing it.

But he didn't know the real reason why she had changed these things about her lifestyle, and if she could help it, he never would.

So, as far as he knew, she just wanted to get away, and Switzerland it was. He planned the trip from beginning to end, booked the flights, reserved the rooms, and even spent extra time with a fancy pants travel agent in Butte planning their complete agenda. He wanted her to see everything she had ever mentioned to him during their late-night talks and mid-day conversations. He knew it wasn't feasible to actually see all there was to see, but he could make sure they visited the places which he knew made up her daydreams. He would spare no expense.

He found himself more and more thankful every day that Silkex had sold the way it had. The initial lump sum purchase amount had allowed them to live in a manner they never would have been able to without it, and ongoing royalties maintained this lifestyle. He was able to continue his work and make sure his princess was living in the manner which she deserved. He couldn't imagine how it was going to be when he finally perfected his formula, but he knew that if he had his way, he would live forever with his beautiful bride, gazing into her eyes and giving her everything she could ever want or need.

But they were getting older; he had to get it worked out soon. He had a dreadful feeling in his soul that if he didn't, it would never be worked out. He felt the odd sensation that he was flying through the air, and his feathers were just about to give out and drop him to the ground. The feeling was enough to take his breath away, and tears nearly sprang to his eyes for no reason.

He pushed the thoughts violently from his mind and continued on a more productive note mentally.

In the meantime, he planned their trip. Neither of them were skiers, so he focused on being able to see sites and do things that didn't involve flying down mountainsides at high rates of speed. The first week they would spend in Zurich, where they would indulge in a variety of activities. They would stay at the Dolder Grand hotel in a luxury suite, and they would spend each of fourteen days there doing different things, all of which he knew would simply sweep his beloved wife off her feet.

One day, they would visit the Zurich Zoo, and the next they would see the Botanical Garden. On day three, they would spend the day strolling Bahnhofstrasse, where they would shop and dine and enjoy all they could see. Day four would be spent at the Swiss National Museum, followed by a visit to Old Town on the fifth day. The sixth day, the day before they would leave for Liechtenstein, they would dine on Lake Zurich, take a walk in a nearby park, then pay a visit to Confeserie Sprungli, where they would enjoy gourmet sweets and desserts.

Day Six would consist of a train ride from Zurich to Liechtenstein, where they would spend the remainder of their trip. There they would stay at the Parkhotel Sonnenhof, where they would visit the national museum, Vaduz Castle, the Main Square, and a variety of other things before spending their last evening, the very night of their forty-fifth anniversary, which they would spend dining by candlelight alone in their room. He would dance with her and tell her how much he had always loved her. Calvin would see to it that by the time they caught their flight back home, she would have no doubt that she was the one and only light of his life, the very thing which drove him on.

With all the essential preparations completed, they left on their flight with stars in their eyes.

∞

About twenty minutes into the air, Calvin turned to

Elaina and asked, "How do you feel, dear?"

She turned to him and squeezed his hand, which held hers gently and lovingly. "Like I am in Heaven with the best-looking man on Earth. What shall we do in Switzerland, Calvin? Tell me now!"

He chuckled, amused by her excited, child-like curiosity. "No, no, you will have to wait and see. Every last bit of it is a surprise, and you shall have to be patient."

Her smile was so broad and her eyes so alight that he swore she was more gorgeous at that moment than any other time since he had known her. His body flushed with the warmth of his love. She was his, and he wanted nothing more than to make her the happiest woman on the planet, forever and ever.

"You do know that I love you, don't you Elaina?"

She turned to him once again, still glowing. "Yes, I do Cal. Do you know that I love you? That I adore you?"

He leaned forward and kissed her briefly, but his kiss was filled with his love, and he made sure she felt it in the softness of his lips and the insistence it conveyed. "I have never been surer of anything in my life, dear."

They settled into the flight then, napping here and there, and eating during the meals. They spent their layovers doing crossword puzzles together and laughing at some of the silly answers they came up with. The flight to Switzerland alone would have been a perfect anniversary, but as it was, it was only the tip of the iceberg.

They arrived in Zurich to find they were in a suite which belonged in a dream. After the bellhop left them, Elaina swirled around in ecstasy, her dress flaring out as she spun around and around. Calvin watched her, fighting the tears of joy which threatened to fall from his eyes. We should have done this years ago, he thought to himself; we should have done this many times over. What was I waiting for? What have I wasted?

But he knew there was no sense in regret; they were there right then, at that moment. They would eat, get some much-needed rest, and get on with making the long-overdue memories he was grieving over. He looked forward to the next two weeks with a swollen heart.

∞

The next day, they officially began their vacation by taking their breakfast on the balcony. Once they had cleaned up and dressed, they headed out for the Zurich Zoo. Calvin was anxious to observe his wife as she took in the animal life there; he was sure that alone would be entertaining.

The zoo did not disappoint. The tigers, elephants, penguins, and a large variety of other breathtaking animals all excited Elaina that once again, she seemed like a child who had just come to life in the world. She giggled and chatted on excitedly about every species they saw, and she ranted about the awesome beauty of the Masoala Rainforest. Calvin made sure to get plenty of photographs; he wanted to have as many as he could of everything and every place. He wanted to be able to reflect, years from now, on the memory of this time.

By the afternoon they were exhausted, so they enjoyed a late lunch and returned to the hotel to rest up in preparation for the next day. Full and warm, the pair retired by seven in the evening, curling up together like newlyweds, with smiles on their faces.

∞

The Botanical Garden, which is where they spent the majority of the following day, didn't have quite the same effect on Elaina as the zoo had. Rather than show childlike excitement, she stood in awe of the beauty exhibited there. She always had loved her garden and flowers. Calvin knew this had been a wonderful choice.

Subsequent visits consisted of shopping and eating at Bahnhofstrasse, The Swiss National Museum, and Old Town, as well as a day out to Lake Zurich and some fancy desserts. The remainder of the time they spent in that area of Switzerland was filled with hand-holding, kisses, laughter, snuggles, and gazing into each other's eyes.

As did their time in Liechtenstein. Every last thing he had planned was more incredible than he could have imagined, and their time at each provided him with feelings he simply could not describe. Calvin Cooper was overwhelmed with his wife, her timeless beauty, and the immense love for her, which filled his heart to overflowing.

It was the final day of their vacation together, and they were dressing for their anniversary dinner, which they would have alone in their room. Cal had ordered five-course meals for them both, each consisting of crab, Porterhouse steaks, fresh seasoned greens, scrumptious portions of pasta, and crusted custards with caramel sauce. They drank cabernet sauvignon together, and they talked over candlelight with Bobby Vinton playing softly over the hi-fi in their room.

They talked about their lives together: old memories from college; the threat of going to jail thanks to the animal activist group, who had no idea what they were talking about or doing. The two of them reflected on the miracles of both Maddie and Noah Carter, and finally, they traded ideas on what the future should hold for them both. As usual, his Elaina insisted that he get home and get his mind back on his work.

All she had ever wanted was for him to be happy, and she stood behind whatever it took to make that happen. All he wanted was to live with her, loving and laughing for all eternity. But something inside of him kept him from voicing that to her yet again. The intuition told him that she would not be receptive to the suggestion even now. Maybe in the future, but not yet, and so he stuck with the dreams which she held for him, and he kept his tongue under control.

At the meal's end, as they enjoyed steaming cups of coffee, Calvin took Elaina's hand and looked at her. Her face was slightly lined, but to him, the lines added to her character. Her hair was graying more than ever, and he noticed it now, but it seemed he never had before. It had been so long since he had really looked at himself; he knew he could never compare with her, and he didn't deserve her. What did people think when they saw this beautiful woman with someone as ragged and worn out as he?

"Elaina, you are so perfect in my eyes," he began, his tone low and his voice filled with love. "What do you see in me? Why do you stay with this old codger?"

As always, she gave a soft laugh. "Oh, Calvin, if only you knew. You are the most handsome man I have ever known. At this point, I don't think that will ever change, my love. You keep getting better and better."

He took her hand and led her to the middle of the room. She buried her face in his chest, and together they swayed to the music. After a moment, she lifted her face and gazed at him. The candlelight lit her eyes, and he could see it dancing with joy in them. He kissed her, a long, soft, luxurious kiss, and then she rested her head on his chest once again.

But suddenly Elaina began to tremble in his arms.

At first, he thought she was crying, but it grew more intense. She took a step back, and her hand went to her forehead. He noticed then that a film of sweat was glistening off her face and bare shoulders. Her eyes fluttered closed, and her breathing became a shallow pant.

"Elaina?"

He knew then that she was going to faint, to hit the

floor hard. He tried to take her by the arm to stop what he clearly saw was happening, but Calvin was a split-second too late. She crumpled to the floor in a heap, a loud sigh escaping her lips.

"Elaina!" Calvin knelt beside her and began to shake her, but she did not respond. "Oh, my, Elaina!"

He raced for the telephone and dialed zero for the front desk. They answered after one ring, much to his relief. "I need a doctor in room 1050 right away! My wife has collapsed and is unconscious on the floor!"

"Room 1050, sir?"

"Yes!" he exclaimed. "Please, hurry!"

Calvin rushed back to Elaina, whose skin had now taken on an ashen hue, and her lips were slightly blue. He jumped up once more and grabbed a cloth napkin off the small dining table. He moistened it in one of the water glasses before returning to her and dabbing it all over her face. He put her head in his lap, and as he tried to cool her, he continued to shake her gently.

"Elaina, you must wake, do you hear what I am saying?" His voice was beginning to sound panicky, and he thought his heart might pound out of his chest. "Now, Elaina! Now!"

A loud knock came at the door, and it was all he could do to tear his attention from his wife long enough to yell, "Come in!" A man with a doctor's bag and a member of the hotel staff came running in.

Calvin gently moved his wife and placed a pillow under her head, then he stepped back to let the doctor work. He watched as the man did all the normal things, and within ten minutes, Elaina's eyes began to flutter, until finally, they were completely open.

"Where? What?" Her voice stuttered slightly, and she sounded confused.

The doctor smiled down at her. "Mrs. Cooper, you are in your hotel room in Liechtenstein. Do you remember?"

She stared at him for a moment, a crease in her brow. After a short bit, her face softened, and she said with a smile, "Yes, yes. Switzerland. It's my forty-fifth anniversary, you know."

The physician laughed and looked up at Calvin. "Forty-five years, yes? Very nice, and congratulations!"

The men helped Elaina to the bed, and then the doctor, who introduced himself as Leon Amstutz, took Calvin into the living area to speak with him in private. The female hotel employee who had accompanied the doctor remained with Elaina to see to it she was comfortable and had everything she needed.

"Mr. Cooper, it seems your wife had a fainting spell," he began, giving Calvin a strange look. "Has she been under much stress, or has she had any nervous problems lately?"

He shook his head. "No. At least, she hasn't spoken of any. This is our last night of a two-week vacation, and she has been fine the entire time."

The man nodded. "Well, it seems she is fine now, but I am unable to say if the spell is perhaps due to some other physical issue. I highly recommend that when you return home, you have her see your regular physician. Let him know what took place and allow him to conduct any testing he requires in order to make a more sound diagnosis. I would say it is likely nothing, but one can never be too sure."

Calvin nodded vigorously. "Absolutely, doctor. I will see to it first thing."

"The best thing for her now is a good rest," Amstutz continued. "And you should encourage her to rest as much as possible on your flight home, even though it is obvious that you are far more virile and energetic than she." He smiled then, gave Calvin a firm pat on the shoulder, and finally left with the hotel employee by his side.

The doctor's statement confused Calvin. Far more virile and energetic? What kind of thing was that for a physician to say to the husband of a patient? Calvin thought it a bit personal, to say the least. He finally concluded that people in Switzerland were simply more personal in their communications, and he chalked the doctor's comment up to be a direct example of that.

When Calvin entered the sleeping room, Elaina was fast asleep, snuggled comfortably under the blankets. She looked peaceful, and her normal color had returned to her face. But none of that was a comfort to him. What had happened tonight? What had caused such a spell? Never before had she done it, and he found the occurrence kept him from sleeping soundly at all.

She looked so old and fragile, he noted as well. Maybe that was what the doctor had meant by his offhand comment. Yes, she was tiny and thin, and even in the middle of her sleep, she looked tired out. The trip had obviously taken its toll on her. He was thankful they had gotten it out of the way now. They would never indulge in such an exhausting luxury again.

It had obviously been too much for his wife to take. She was too tired to be traveling such a distance. And all the activity had nearly done her in!

He would make sure to take Elaina to see Dr. Bergstrom immediately upon their return home.

CHAPTER 11

The airplane cut gently through the blue sky, heading back to America with eager, if not exhausted, passengers. At least Calvin could vouch that both he and Elaina were two of them. Right at that moment, she slept peacefully next to him, head resting against the wall on a pillow the stewardess had provided her with. As she slept, he looked her over with great concern, and he reflected on the conversation they had shortly after takeoff.

She had been the same sweet woman she always was, making sure he was comfortable and had everything he needed before she would even consider her own needs. He had yet to bring up the fainting incident from the night before, and he hadn't intended to bring it up until they were settled in back at home, but as he watched her fuss over him, he became frustrated. Was this selflessness the reason she passed out? Was she so anxious ridden over him all the time that it finally caught up with her? He could keep his silence no longer.

"Elaina, when we get home, I would like you to make an appointment to see Dr. Bergstrom," he began.

"I am very concerned over your health."

She didn't respond to him at all; not even so much as a nod.

"Dear, did you hear what I said?" he asked.

She fluffed her pillow, put it between the plane wall and her head, and said, "Mmm-hmm."

Calvin could feel the frustration mounting inside of him. She seemed so complacent as if she had no concern whatsoever regarding what had happened. For him, the thought of losing her stirred up a feeling much like what he would imagine suffocating to feel like, and he didn't appreciate her careless attitude.

"You know, I would certainly expect a yes or no answer," he continued in a low voice. "Actually, a 'yes' would be nice."

Elaina lifted her head and looked at him with unflinching eyes. "Calvin, I feel fine. I'm sure it was the elevation or some other simple thing. I am not going to waste Hal Bergstrom's time, and that is all I have to say about that."

Her voice was short, and her tone was sharp, though she did keep her voice low as well. Never before had she spoken to him in such a manner, and it caused him to feel a bit of alarm. Why was she so adamant? If it was nothing, she should be willing to appease him by paying a brief visit to the physician. After all, they could certainly afford it, so what was the problem?

He had watched her for a while longer before finally putting his head back and closing his eyes. He wanted to hash out the issue right then and there, but that wouldn't do, considering they were surrounded by other passengers. No, he would have to force himself to be patient and deal with his own confusion and frustration. Elaina hated the negative attention of others, hated the very thought of bickering or fighting in public. If he pushed the issue right then, she would certainly have his hide when they got home, and he would never live it down.

She would never give in and take the formula if he made her angry and pushed her.

So, he spent the first leg of the flight squirming and worrying, and he got no sleep at all. By the time they finished their last layover and boarded their final flight, he was beside himself with concern, and all he wanted to do was get home and deal with things.

But Elaina slept fine the entire trip. Even during the layover, she seemed to not have the slightest thought about what had happened. He couldn't figure it out. Nothing about her behavior was normal, nothing at all.

Dependable old Ralph was there to pick them up, just as they expected. Elaina sat in the back seat and said very little, but her disposition was pleasant and upbeat. Calvin kept up appearances with his assistant by telling him of all they did during their vacation and giving him amusing little details about the different places they visited and the things they saw.

They were home by three o'clock that afternoon.

"Ralph, why don't you go on out to the lab," Calvin stated. "I'm going to make sure Elaina doesn't need any help unpacking the luggage, then I will come out, and you can fill me in on any progress you have made on the dosages."

Ralph agreed easily and left the house, so Calvin made his way into the bedroom. "Elaina, I want to discuss why you won't go see Dr. Bergstrom."

She had her back to him, unpacking his suitcase and separating the clean clothes from the dirty ones. "There is nothing to discuss."

All he could do was stare at her in disbelief. She continued to focus on the task at hand, and after a couple of minutes, he simply turned on his heel and left the room, shutting the door hard behind him.

Once the door was closed, Elaina turned around and sat down hard on the bed. She breathed a sigh of relief and put her head in her hands. Lord, she hoped she didn't have to deal with this issue every time she was alone with her husband. This was truly the last thing she needed.

Yes, the fainting spell in Liechtenstein had been the most severe spell yet. Mostly they were only dizzy spells, and she was always alone when they occurred. Now Calvin had been witness to one of them, and it just happened to be one that brought her to the ground unconscious. Yes, she was a bit concerned.

But the fact was, if she were to give in and see the doctor, and something was truly wrong, Calvin's focus would be on her and her alone, and she knew it. No, that was unacceptable. She would not be a burden on him.

So, she decided that she would see Hal Bergstrom,

but she would do it alone. That way, if something was wrong, she could deal with it on her own, at least, she could until she was no longer able. But maybe it was minor, and she didn't need to be putting up such a fight.

Elaina reached over and picked up the telephone receiver from the nightstand. She dialed Dr. Bergstrom's number.

She made an appointment for the following morning and decided that she wouldn't tell Calvin about it unless everything was okay. If not, well, she would figure out what to do when the time came. He was her husband, though, and no matter what, she needed to respect his wishes in the end, as long as they were reasonable.

But regardless of how things came out, she would never, ever turn to the formula.

∞

Calvin spent a solid three hours in the laboratory being caught up on things Ralph had been working on with the formula. As expected, there had been no progress. If Calvin was stuck trying to figure out the concentration and its strength, he certainly couldn't expect miracles from his assistant.

It was time to get back to work and focus on the formula. It was still too weak, and the administration amounts were too much, unless one was a horse. It was pointless to continue with the rats, however, so Calvin and Ralph decided to go to the humane society in Randalia and adopt a couple of old dogs who were on their last legs. They would usually eat just about anything, so that struggle would be eliminated, and any success would be easy to see and measure due to their old age, just as Maddie's had been.

As for Maddie, Calvin decided he would cut her dosage down by one-third and see if her progress was maintained. It was time to get serious about perfecting his product. He suspected that Elaina may be ill, and he wanted to be sure to have things right for her. That wasn't to say she would take it willingly, and he would never force her, but if she would, he wanted to be ready.

So, Calvin prepared to get back to his normal day to day life, but his beautiful wife wore heavy on his mind. He dealt with it as he dealt with everything having to do with life, pain, and reality: he ignored it. He pushed it out of his mind. She was still young, and she had another twenty or thirty years left on her. By then, he would certainly be able to convince her to take the formula, especially if he perfected it.

It continued to drive him.

He would be her salvation. He would heal her if she ever got sick. It was that simple. She was stubborn now, but that would change if the reality of her own mortality ever looked her in the eye, he was sure of it.

So, for the hundredth time, Calvin focused on his work.

CHAPTER 12

"Well, Elaina, I have to admit," Dr. Bergstrom was saying, "I can't second guess what happened to you in Switzerland, but I can tell you what my thoughts are now that I have seen you."

Elaina sat in a cushioned chair across from the man's desk, looking at him and waiting patiently. He had given her a full head-to-toe check-up and had taken blood as well. He told her it would be a week before her blood test results came back, but he could make a short-term diagnosis for the time being.

"In my professional opinion you are simply tired and nervous, and I believe you have been letting this go on for far too long," he stated in a matter-of-fact tone.

Elaina looked down at her purse and began to fiddle with the straps. "Dr. Bergstrom, I don't feel nervous, and I'm not tired. I get around easily enough; I mean, I'm active around the house, and I work in the garden, but I have someone come to help with the heavier labor."

"Good," he said. "I'm glad to hear it. Are you taking vitamins?"

She shook her head.

"Well," he replied as he began to scribble on a prescription pad, "I am going to order a prescription for a multi-vitamin, and I am also going to give you a mild tranquilizer, Valium. Now, it shouldn't put you to sleep, but it will take the edge off. You should notice a huge difference if indeed stress is the problem."

He signed both prescriptions with flare, and as he handed them to her, he said, "Now, no driving on the Valium; make sure you stay home when you take it unless Calvin or Ralph is driving, okay?"

She smiled and nodded at him as she took the slips of paper, which she tucked into her purse.

"If your blood work comes back abnormal in any way, I will give you a call," he continued. "Otherwise, consider no news to be good news. And if you have any more problems or concerns, I want you to make another appointment, agreed?"

"Yes, thank you." She stood from her chair and shook Hal Bergstrom's hand, then he walked her out to the waiting room.

"Do me a favor," he said. "Make sure you tell those two boys hello for me, would you? I don't get to visit with Cal half as much as I'd like to."

"Sure thing," she said with a smile, and she left his office feeling much lighter.

Elaina stopped at the pharmacy and had her prescriptions filled before heading home. On the drive back she thought about what Hal had said: nerves. She was relieved that all she had to report to her husband was nerves, and he would be glad that she had given in and made the appointment.

But nagging at the back of her mind was the blood test. Something inside of her was unsettled over the whole thing. She tried to push it out of her mind and focus on other thoughts, but it stayed there in her brain, tugging and yanking, weighing heavy on her heart.

Deep inside, she knew. She knew that her body was telling her that nothing was right, nothing was ever going to be the same again. There was something dreadfully wrong, no matter what Dr. Bergstrom said about her checkup. No, her heart knew what her mind was denying. It would do no good to fret over it now; she would worry about it when the time came.

But, for today, she could report to her husband the truth; she would just leave the part about the blood test out.

∞

The following Wednesday, Elaina was in the kitchen preparing supper for herself, Calvin, and Ralph. She didn't know why she made so much food anymore; she never had an appetite. But Cal watched her so closely, so to make only enough for the two of them would give that fact away, and she wasn't willing to do that.

She glanced at the clock on the wall: four-fifteen. She was just getting into the swing of the meal preparation now, so it wouldn't be complete until nearly six. That would be fine with her; it would give her a bit more time alone, in the quiet and still of the house. Her head ached slightly, just as it had for the past couple of days. She had taken just about all the acetaminophen that she could handle, so all she could do was hope and pray that it didn't get any worse. She was just tired of it aching.

She placed a casserole dish filled with au gratin potatoes in the oven, and just as she closed the door, the telephone rang.

"Hello?"

A woman's voice responded. "Hello? I am trying to reach the Cooper residence. Is this Elaina Cooper?"

"Why, yes," she replied. "Yes, it is."

"Mrs. Cooper, this is Katherine from Dr. Bergstrom's office," the woman continued. "The doctor wanted me to let you know that we have received the results from your blood work back, and he would like to see you to discuss those results. I am calling to arrange an appointment for you."

Elaina's heart began to pound. "Well, you have me on the phone now," she replied. "Can't you just fill me in?"

"I'm sorry, Mrs. Cooper," Katherine said regretfully. "It is our policy that all test results be discussed in person, and only Dr. Bergstrom is allowed by law to do that. When will you have some free time to come in, ma'am?"

Elaina closed her eyes and kept still for a moment. Dr. Bergstrom had told her that no news was good news, so she could only assume that this was the opposite. She had to calm herself before she spoke, because she felt like crying.

"Mrs. Cooper?"

"Yes, Katherine, I'm here," she said quickly. She opened her eyes and looked at the calendar which hung next to the phone, though she had no reason to do so. Elaina had no upcoming appointments or obligations whatsoever, and she knew it. "Any time is fine."

"Well, he would like you to come in as soon as possible," the woman continued. "How about tomorrow morning at eight-thirty? Would that work for you?"

"Yes, yes dear," she said in a low voice. "I'll be there. See you then."

Elaina hung up the phone gently without even waiting for the woman to say goodbye. She leaned her forehead against the wall once again, her hands trembling. What was she going to say to Calvin? If he knew she had an appointment, he would want to go with her, and she hadn't mentioned anything to him about the blood tests. But then again, she was going to have to tell him sooner or later no matter what.

No, she would go alone. She would tell him whatever she learned when she returned, and if he were angry that she had not told him everything, she would simply explain her reasons honestly. She would not take him from his work to go with her to the doctor. She could do it alone.

With that, Elaina stood tall. She walked to the kitchen sink and splashed water on her face, then patted it dry with the hand towel which hung from the strap of her apron. She put a smile on her face, ignored the nagging pain in her head, and concentrated on supper preparations.

No need to stir herself up; tomorrow morning would come soon enough.

∞

"Elaina, your test results show both a low white cell count as well as some abnormal cells," Dr. Bergstrom was saying. "In my experience, this is a sure sign of something called chronic myeloid leukemia." He held up his hand. "Now, before you get excited, this is something that I, myself, do not feel comfortable diagnosing on my own. I am a general practitioner, but I have had a couple of patients in the past with similar forms. I am referring you to an oncologist in Butte. He is a wonderful man with years and years of experience both diagnosing and treating these cancer forms."

She simply stared at him. His mouth was moving, and words were coming out, but he sounded as if he were speaking to her through a pillow. She nodded now and then as he spoke, but she was not actively involved in the conversation at all. The only thing on her mind was Calvin.

"I want you to get into him as soon as possible," Hal Bergstrom was saying. "So I have had Katherine make an appointment for you for tomorrow at eleven in the morning."

He handed her a card across his desk. "You must make this appointment, Elaina."

She reached up and took the card from him, glanced at it, and tucked it into the front pocket of her purse before turning her attention back to him.

"Do you have any questions for me, dear?"

She simply shook her head.

Dr. Bergstrom stared at her in silence for a moment. "Listen, I realize this is so, so much to be handed at once. Surely Calvin is supporting you well recently. He will be strong with you, regardless of what you are facing. I know he adores you."

"He doesn't know."

Bergstrom creased his brow. "What do you mean, 'he doesn't know'? About the dizziness?"

She shook her head, embarrassed. "He didn't know I came to see you. I mean, he wanted me to, he told me to, but I told him no. I told him I would be fine, and he let it go." She reached into her purse and pulled out a crisp white handkerchief, which she dabbed at the corners of her eyes with before beginning to twist it nervously in her hands. "Even after I saw you, I didn't tell him. I told him I went shopping, and I didn't mention anything about the blood tests."

"Elaina, you have to tell him," Hal continued firmly. "Especially now. You will need him more than ever. You must go straight home and tell your husband what is happening, do you understand?"

Elaina nodded and offered the doctor a grim smile. "Is there anything else, Hal?"

He shook his head and stood up, then walked around the desk and sat in the empty chair next to her. He put his arm around her shoulders and leaned toward her. "There is no more time for you to be concerned about Calvin's welfare, Elaina. I know, I know. I've known you two for years, and his hopes and dreams have always been the priority for you. But if you keep this from him, well, it will break his heart. It's time for him to be your husband, do you understand?"

She nodded yet again and was beginning to feel like one of those dashboard decorations which sat in cars and bounced around.

"Now, I want you to go home and take care of this," he continued. "Next, I want you and your husband to get to Butte tomorrow and see Dr. Alan Maschmann. He is a wonderful, compassionate man, and he is a leader in his field. Katherine has copied some driving instructions for you, so be sure to get those from her on your way out."

Elaina stood up, and so did he. He stood before her, concern all over his face. She held out her hand so he could shake it, but he ignored the gesture and gave her a hug instead.

After a moment he stepped back and leaving his hands on her shoulders, looked her in the eye and said, "Let me know what's happening. Keep me posted, and if Cal needs to talk, ever, at any time, either one of you, please call me."

She nodded and smiled again, a robot just going through the motions. In the waiting room, she fetched the instructions from Katherine, who continued to give her a look she could only construe as pity. She hoped the woman wouldn't say anything to her, but she knew that wouldn't be so.

"You are in my prayers, Mrs. Cooper."

Another smile, another nod. "Thank you, dear."

Two minutes later, she was unlocking the Buick. She calmly tossed her purse over to the passenger seat, then got in and shut the door just as it began to rain. Elaina sat there, watching the drops hit the windshield, sporadically at first, then harder and faster until it was pouring. The windows began to fog over, and finally, she let go. She began to sob uncontrollably, her shoulders heaving, her face dripping wet with her tears. She made no sound, though. She simply cried harder than she had ever cried in her life, and she did it for about ten minutes.

That was when the rain eased up a bit, and that was when she started the car and turned on the defroster. When the windows were clear, Elaina put the car in reverse and backed out of her parking spot. She pulled out of the lot and into the street traffic, and from there she headed home, calm, cool, and collected.

CHAPTER 13

1994

The dream life in paradise, led by Calvin and Elaina Cooper, would never be the same again.

It had been four years since that fateful day when she had sat, frozen, in Dr. Bergstrom's office, listening to his soundless droning. Four years since she had sat in the Buick in the rain, sobbing her eyes out. Yet not for herself, but for her sweet, sweet Calvin.

Calvin, the grown man who could hardly take care of himself. Calvin, the scientific genius who was able to make miracles happen, but couldn't manage to comb his own hair. Calvin, who forgot to take in proper nourishment for days on end, but worried sick about how much other people were eating.

Beautiful, perfect, loving Calvin.

∞

She had collected herself quickly that day in the car. She had driven herself home with all the confidence of a woman without a care in the world, a woman who didn't have a worry for tomorrow. Elaina Cooper had wiped her eyes, smiled, turned on the radio, and began to hum as she steered that big beast of a car out of

Randalia, past Twixt, and into her driveway. She had parked, gone into the house, freshened up, and proceeded to use the telephone to call out to the lab and ask her husband to come inside for a chat.

She would never forget his face when he had walked through the front door. She had been sitting at the dining room table, two cups of steaming coffee prepared, and a box of tissue strategically placed near where Calvin would sit. She was done crying; it was time to take care of him for a bit. After all, soon she wouldn't be able to, and it was the thing she loved most in life.

He was smiling. He had kissed her and then sat down, rambling on and on about his incessant struggles with the formula. She had listened quietly as she always had, her full attention on the beautiful male seated with her.

Finally, he had turned to her. "Enough about me. What did you want to speak with me about, dear?"

As soon as he spoke those words, her face had changed. She felt it, but she had been powerless to do anything about it. He noticed immediately, just as she had known he would. His smile had flown from his face.

"Elaina, what is it?"

So, she let it spill out, and spill out it did, in great waves and gusts like so much vomit. She started by telling him that the dizzy spells had been going on for a while. She admitted to him that she had gone to Dr. Bergstrom the week before, after they had returned from Switzerland, just as he had wanted her to. Then she told him about the blood test, Bergstrom's suspicions, and her appointment in Butte the following morning.

At first, he tried to brush it off. Oh, he said, it could be anything. Bergstrom was a small-town doctor; he couldn't be sure. It could be the final fringes of menopause, exhaustion, old age. Elaina had let him go on and on, a calm smile on her face.

After about twenty minutes, he slowed down long enough to search her face, desperately, and ask her, "Couldn't it be? Elaina, couldn't it be?"

She had simply continued to smile and gently shook her head.

Next, he had gotten angry. He paced and shook his fist. He called the doctor, his good friend, a liar, and accused him of trying to steal his wife away. Next, he began to admit there may be a slight problem, but it would be minor, and the doctors in Butte would give her a few shots, and she would be fine.

Next, he began to sob. He fell on the floor at her feet and buried his face in her lap. He cried for so long that he ran out of breath and tears. After that, he calmed himself and went into the bathroom. When he emerged, his eyes were rimmed with red, and his nose was running.

"You will begin the formula," he had said.

Elaina shook her head and said in a soft voice, "No, Calvin."

"Yes!" He demanded. "You will begin the formula, and it will heal you, and we will go on with our lives."

"I don't want to live forever, Cal," she insisted. "I will not take the formula."

He sat back down, his eyes desperate. "Please. It will work!"

Elaina had taken a deep breath and crossed her arms over her chest to let him know she meant what she said. "I will let the doctors treat me, but only to an extent. If taking chemo means I will lose my hair, or be sick often, I will not do that either. I will die here, in our home, in our bed, on my terms.

I do not want to live forever. If this is my time, it is my time, Calvin."

He had stared at her in disbelief. Here, he had the means to turn back time, to literally erase the years and their damaging effects. But his wife, the woman who had loved him and endlessly supported his work, refused to let him help her.

"Elaina –"

"That's my final word, my love."

He had stood up, angry, and stormed out of the house. Elaina spoke a short prayer, asking the Lord to help Calvin accept life on life's terms for once in his life, and then she stood and went about her chores. She would not change her mind, and she was going to enjoy what time she had left.

∞

Now it was four years later, and she and Calvin were sitting at the Butte Cancer Specialists Center for the hundredth time. Dr. Maschmann had been treating her since the diagnosis and the confirmation, but little had stopped the progression of the sickness.

She had Chronic Myeloid Leukemia, a cancer of the blood. It entailed much, and though she had been educated fairly well, she could truly say she didn't care about the ins and outs. The only reason she was going this far was for Calvin. Today she would be told what the doctors would recommend next in her treatment, but she would refuse if it were to make her feel sick, or weak, or bald.

First, they had used a couple of different approaches: they had changed her diet and put her on various mild medications but to no avail. That had lasted for nearly three years. After a while she was obviously worsening, so they decided to move on.

Next, she was given a form of chemotherapy which doctors said would not make her nauseous and her hair should remain intact. But, unfortunately, the treatment exhausted her. She did it for a year before finally refusing to go any further.

Now she was waiting for their next offering, but she was sure she knew what was coming, and so did Calvin. He wanted her to begin whatever they wanted her to, but she stood her ground. He had continuously tried to change her mind about the formula, and finally, she had blown up at him, something she had never done before. That had been a month ago, and he hadn't brought it up since.

Cal was unable to focus on his work like before due to her appointments, so Ralph had taken over as best as he could, but no progress was truly being made. Elaina found herself often wishing it was over so he could go on and live again. He was strong; he may falter for a bit, but he would find his footing again.

"Elaina Cooper."

A young nurse, pretty and blond, was calling her name, a chart in her hands. Elaina touched Calvin's arm, and together they followed the nurse back to the exam rooms.

She went through the normal process. Vitals, how was she feeling? Any new symptoms? What was the doctor seeing her about today? She answered everything pleasantly and thoroughly, while her husband stewed quietly, from the chair next to hers.

They waited for another half-hour before Dr. Maschmann entered the room.

"Hello, you two," he began as he scanned her chart. "Looks like things have pretty much remained the same, I see."

Elaina nodded yes, and he continued.

"So, today I am going to present you with your next option," he said. "Now, I know you have been resistant in the past, but I want you to know that for the negative side effects, this treatment has a pretty good success rate, Mrs. Cooper."

"Bone marrow transplant followed by chemo?"

He nodded. "Yes. Stronger than before. The treatment we usually turn to in… at this phase."

Her grin broadened. He had almost said 'in the end.' She felt amused.

"Hair? Vomiting?"

Dr. Maschmann looked down at the chart in his hands. "Unfortunately, yes. But it all passes once the treatment is over."

"No, thank you doctor."

Calvin stood up and left the room.

Maschmann cleared his throat. "Elaina, this is our last hope. Aside from this, your other option is for us to write you medications to make you comfortable, and send you home. You do realize that, don't you? Is that really what you want? What about Calvin?"

"Calvin has been aware of my feelings about this from the very beginning," she said. "He doesn't have to like it. This is my choice. So, how long do I have with the treatment?"

Maschmann shrugged. "If it is successful, several years if it doesn't recur."

"What is the rate?" she asked.

He cleared his throat. "For a woman your age, about fifty-fifty, maybe less. But, it does work in some cases. Many believe it is worth the risk."

She had done the research. It was a very painful and sickening process. It would be harder on Cal to watch her go through it than it would be to let nature take its course.

Maschmann continued with a concerned look. "Based on your blood work, I would say you have a little over one year."

Elaina stood her ground.

"No, doctor. Thank you for all you do, but no."

He nodded, his eyes still glued to the cover of the

chart. "Do me a favor, Elaina. Continue to give it thought, okay? I'll adjust and refill your medication. You go home and take as long as you need. If you change your mind, I am always just a phone call away."

"Thank you," she said.

He stood. "Oh, yes," he continued. He pulled a card out of his pocket. "Here is the number of a… therapist. Just in case Calvin has a difficult time adjusting."

Elaina stood and took the card with her trademark smile. She hugged the man for the hundredth time, then put her coat on. Finally, she turned to him.

"Can I go?"

"Yes. Just wait for your prescriptions," he stated. "About ten or fifteen minutes. They'll call your name at the desk when they're ready."

As she walked alone down the hall to the reception area, she realized she felt free for the first time in years. Free of the pressure put on her by the medical professionals; free of the pressure her husband put on her. The choice was hers, and she had made it. Solidly and certainly, she had made her decision.

∞

So Elaina Cooper began to get comfortable at home for the first time, as well.

Calvin spent a few weeks very angry, and he stayed out in the lab with Ralph as much as he could. Ralph and Elaina had many talks; he understood her point of view, and he supported her decision. He tried to discuss it with Calvin, but her husband wouldn't hear it.

But she went on anyway, and finally, after about six

months, Calvin slowly but surely began to accept reality and come around. It was a huge relief to her because she became a bit more tired each and every day. She also began to deal with worsening symptoms.

Nosebleeds, something she had a few times here and there, began to come quite often. Most of the time she just dealt with them, but a few times, Calvin actually had to help her to bed and clean things up. Once he started to accept her decision, as well as the true process of life and death when it was out of his hands, all of that didn't matter. Things began to get easier and more peaceful again.

Their fiftieth anniversary was in 1995, and by then, Calvin and Elaina Cooper were actually laughing together again. Elaina knew by that time that she would die peacefully. Now, her only prayer for her husband was that he would come to realize what she already knew: reversing age and sickness wasn't the answer. As a matter of fact, it would cause far more pain than it would ever heal.

For their anniversary, they watched a couple of movies on cable television, and they ordered Chinese take-out from Randalia, which Calvin had to drive to pick up. Ralph spent a few hours with them that evening before retiring, just as they had invited him to. Afterward, the couple played a couple of games of Gin Rummy, something they hadn't done together in years.

At the end of the day, as they lay in their bed holding each other, Elaina thanked him for the best anniversary she had ever had, bar none.

She was an angel of light and mercy. She had supported his dreams, and she didn't even agree with them. What she knew was that she loved him, and what she wanted or needed to prove to him didn't matter.

She knew a lot, Elaina Cooper did. Far more than even her genius husband. No, she didn't know formulas or the periodic table very well, but the things she did know about were the things in life that really mattered. She knew that what was temporary was really permanent in the end. Things like love, and life.

As Calvin held her that night, realizing that she was really and truly going to die, he had contemplated slipping her the formula without her knowing. Surely she wouldn't be angry at him when her pain was gone, and her eyes were clear, especially when they could see each new anniversary together. Surely, she would thank him.

But even as he thought about it, he knew that he never would. To do so would be for him to betray her very trust, and never once, in all their years of marriage, had she done so to him. Sure, she had fibbed about the blood test, but that had been to save him pain.

The fact was that, even as he fought the temptation to do it, it still gripped his heart and occupied his mind. It would be easy, he told himself. Just put it in her food...

But the choice would not have been hers, and that would have made him as bad as those people from AFRAIDS had accused him of being all those years ago. It would mean he was doling out abuse. It would mean he was practicing the scientific arts unethically.

He lay there, holding her, and he felt his eyes beginning to sting with the tears of losing her while she was still alive. One crept out of his eye and slid down his cheek onto his pillow. In the moonlight, he could see her thin, sick face, and he was angry with God. He was furious. What right did He have to take away the only good thing that Calvin had ever known or loved?

The thought came to him: what right do you have to play God?

That was exactly what he had been doing for the majority of his life, and while he felt ashamed, he was still not willing to give up his dream. He was still not willing to close the books and walk away. He wanted to stop the sting of death in its tracks for everyone in the future. No one, ever or anywhere, should feel the way he was feeling right then.

He wouldn't sleep well that night, or for many nights afterward. No, he had created a monster. He had brought it to life. The monster was he…

R.W.K. Clark

CHAPTER 14

1996

Calvin Cooper sat still, his legs stretched out before him, sleeping soundly in the soft reclining chair that he had moved into the bedroom when his wife became bed-ridden. A book was sprawled open, face-down on his chest, and his head leaned peacefully against one of the wingbacks on the chair. He slept soundly, a slight snore emanating from him, which was hardly audible.

Calvin's wife of more than fifty years, Elaina, was lying on the bed next to him. She was gazing at him lovingly, a slight smile on her face. Her skin was gray and pale, and her eyes seemed to have sunk into her head. Her hair, which was as white as snow, was also as thin as paper. But even with all of this, one could tell that there had been a time when Elaina Cooper had been a breathtakingly beautiful woman, for the ghost of her beauty still danced across her face.

Elaina coughed and, unable to get it under control, began to practically choke. She shook violently and struggled to catch her breath. It became harder and harder to breathe anymore, but what could one expect from a very sick old woman?

She tried to sit up, but her strength was sapped. After only seconds of coughing, Calvin was roused, and he sat forward quickly, his book dropping to the floor, forgotten. Panic was written all over his face as he reached forward to help her achieve a more erect position.

"Elaina, I'm here," Calvin said lovingly as he gently pulled her forward. He began to pat her on the shoulder as if trying to softly beat the cough from her body. After only a moment of sitting upright, Elaina was able to gain control of her cough, and she looked at her husband and smiled once again.

"Thank you, dear."

Calvin slowly lowered her back down onto her pillow, then sat back in the chair again. "I must have dozed off, my love," he said. "I'm sorry. It seems I am a bit worn out. Certainly don't last as long as I used to, do I Elaina?"

He reached out and took her hand, his eyes searching her face. "I have done nothing but work and work and work. What did you ever see in this crazy old man, anyway?"

She gave him a weak chuckle, and her frail hand squeezed his, but just barely. Calvin saw that her eyes were a bit glazed, almost detached, and it caused him to sit forward. "Are you okay, my dear?"

Elaina nodded only once. "What did I see?" she asked. "What do I see?" Now her eyelids fluttered quickly, and Calvin just… knew.

"You always were the most beautiful man I have

ever known, my love," she replied. "Make me one promise: look in the mirror…"

When her spirit left her body a fraction of a second later, Calvin could almost see it, and he was sure that he felt it. "Elaina?" His thumb stroked her hand as he said it again and again. "Elaina? Elaina?"

She was gone. He leaned forward and brushed his palm over her eyes, closing them once and for all, then he sat back, her hand firmly in his. Tears fell from his eyes, slowly at first, but soon they picked up speed. Calvin let them fall, but the rest of his body sat still. He never had been dramatic about emotional pain or grief, even though right at that moment he felt as if he were dying.

He would have to call Dr. Bergstrom to come and take care of the details, but for the time being, he wanted to simply sit quietly with his wife. He wanted to think about all that she was, and all that she had been. He wanted to simply feel her skin as it cooled. He wanted to tell her, over and over, what she meant to him and how much he adored her.

For the next hour, Calvin sat next to his wife, weeping and reminiscing about their beautiful life together. It could not have been any more perfect than it was. They had been two peas in a pod.

Calvin was a scientist, and his primary focus had been health and the prolonging of life itself. Some teased him, saying he was nearly mad with obsession, and he would have to agree with them. He never brushed his hair or bothered with his appearance, and that fact made him definitely look like he was out of his mind. As a matter of fact, Calvin didn't look in the mirror... ever. He saw no point in it, and he even went so far as to look at the floor if he so much as passed a mirror or any other reflective surface.

The truth was, Calvin thought he was... funny looking, and he thought more so as he began to near forty, so right around that time he stopped using mirrors. Elaina never failed to tell him what a 'beautiful man' he was; as a matter of fact, she told him constantly, and it helped his ego to keep its head above the proverbial waters. She would gaze at him as if he were simply perfect, and stroke his cheeks with her hands. He loved it, and it was all he ever needed.

Calvin let go of Elaina's cooling hand hesitantly and picked up the receiver of the telephone. He dialed Dr. Bergstrom's home number, recalling it from memory. The man had become such a regular part of their daily lives that he and the good doctor called each other 'friends.'

It was two o'clock in the morning, Calvin noted with a glance at the clock on the nightstand. He thought about hanging up and calling back at dawn, but right then Hal Bergstrom picked up the line.

"This is Dr. Bergstrom." His voice was ragged with sleep.

Calvin took a deep breath. "Hal, this is Calvin. I'm afraid it's time."

Bergstrom was silent for only a moment before replying, "I'll be there shortly."

After hanging up, Calvin looked lovingly at Elaina, then he pulled the bedspread up and covered her peaceful face with it. She was so gorgeous, even in her old age. He had worked so hard to find a way to make them both young forever but to no avail. The truth was, he had wasted all of his time, time that he could have been spending with his precious, patient, and understanding wife.

Now there was no time left.

What were her last words to him? He pondered this with a smile on his face. He had asked her what she had ever seen in him, and she had replied with honesty, as always.

"What did I see? What do I see? You have always been the most beautiful man I have ever known, my love."

The smile faded from Calvin's face. Love, indeed, was blind. Calvin knew that he was definitely not beautiful in anyone's eyes but Elaina's. He stood, shaking his head, and for the first time in decades went to the mirror.

He stood at Elaina's dresser looking down at her things. Her hairbrush and comb sat there, looking as though they missed her already. He noticed her perfume bottles and her face powder. It broke his heart to look, but even right then he realized it was easier than looking at himself in the mirror. Finally, Calvin Cooper forced his eyes upward, and he nearly fell backward at what he saw.

He didn't look a day over forty... not a day.

Calvin turned quickly to his wife, only to see her covered body. He was very confused. He looked back at the mirror in wonder and raised his hand to his skin. Yes, it was real; Calvin Cooper looked as if he hadn't aged a day since he stopped looking in the mirror.

He staggered backward, his eyes glued to his reflection until the backs of his legs hit the chair, and he sat down hard. Something in his work had done this; something he had done had caused all of his trials and experiments to actually work.

Now she was gone, and she left, like smoke out an open window on a breezy summer night. He stood before his wife, hating himself for not defying her and saving her anyway.

She had known all along. Poor Elaina, she had been married to a man who looked young enough to be her son. Suddenly, Calvin was able to recall the glances and backhanded whispers of those they encountered in public. He all of a sudden remembered funny glances in Switzerland, and the way that Dr. Bergstrom would nod, condescendingly, when he would speak to Calvin and Elaina. What had she and the doctor spoke of when they were alone? Had she shared the details of Calvin's studies?

Of course she had, and true to form, Dr. Bergstrom had held it in the strictest of confidence. Calvin felt sick, but it was misdirected. He didn't feel sick at all for what he might be thinking he put Elaina through. No. He felt sick that she wouldn't take the formula, so she could be alive with him today. She wouldn't even try the Waba to make it taste better.

It was at that very moment that he knew. It came to him like an avalanche might come to a naked man standing powerless at the foot of a snow-covered mountain. All those years he spent isolating and extracting proteins and compounds; all that time he spent trying to figure out how to minimize the formula's dosage, when all along it had been this simple.

It was the Waba paste, and just like that, he realized any thought that might have put his mind right, went straight out the window. He was a genius and an accomplished one at that. But Calvin Cooper was on the verge of being a mad scientist.

Elaina had always told him she thought he was beautiful, and he was sure that in her eyes he was. Yes, perhaps the original formula he had created from all the fruits and vegetables had played a part in his somewhat youthful appearance all those years ago, for she certainly let him know he looked great. But now, standing there and staring at his own reflection, there was no doubt in his mind that something had played a much bigger part in what he saw than a bunch of pomegranates, grapes, and berries.

Yes… it was the Waba.

Now it was time for him to do something about all of this. Never again would anyone be forced to feel the way he felt at that moment: the loss, the emptiness, the unbearable pain of losing his Elaina. He was going to see to it that no one ever had to suffer this way again if they didn't want to. The human race, with all of its intelligence and ability, should have the choice to live as long as they possibly could, and they should look and feel like a million bucks while doing it. It was time.

∞

The first thing Calvin Cooper did was find a new place to live and work. He couldn't bear the thought of staying in Montana, not without Elaina. Everywhere he looked, everything he touched and smelled, took his mind to her, and with the memories came that deep, untouchable longing which threatened to tear out his soul and leave him lifeless.

He sat Ralph down and had a long talk with him. He told him how he felt and what he intended to do. Of course, he asked Ralph if he wanted to join him, and Calvin was sure that his long-time assistant would do just that. But Cal was in for a big surprise.

"Calvin, you know, I'm older than you are," the man told him. "And… and since Elaina has been sick and we haven't been working as much, I have been seeing someone."

Calvin's eyes grew wide. "You have? Well, who is she? You could bring her! She could support us in our work. Ralph, this is going to change the world; it is going to make Calvin Cooper and Ralph Gordon household names."

Ralph took a deep breath, and for the first time in a very long time, maybe ever, Calvin got a good look at his old friend and helper. The man had very little hair left. His eyes had grown so dim that the lenses of his glasses were three times as thick as they were when they had met. He was as thin as a rail, and his hands shook terribly.

"How old are you now, Ralph?" Calvin asked.

Ralph chuckled. "I'm seventy-eight, Cal. Seventy-eight."

Calvin sat back hard in his chair. He should've known that; he was a scientist, for goodness' sake. He could've done the math. Of course, the man wanted to take it easy.

But Calvin was still missing it. He was still caught up in his hopes and dreams and goals, and he was missing it. His wife was gone, and she had refused the formula. Here sat his workmate; maybe he will be willing to take it, Calvin thought.

"Do you want to use the formula?"

Ralph chuckled yet again and shook his head. "I have no interest in becoming young again. My years are earned... I bought and paid for. They are mine, and I don't want anyone to take them from me, much less give them away for free. I want to build a life with Irene. I want to find a home, get married, and settle down. I want to die with someone in a place I can call my own. Do you understand?"

He sounds like Elaina, Calvin thought, and though he truly didn't understand, he could let the man make his own choices, just like his wife had. Yes, he was ambitious; some would even call him an unrealistic dreamer, but Calvin Cooper was no thief. Yet for all his genius, he was still missing it.

Cal stood up and began to pace. "How about if you

stay here. You can have the house, keep Maddie if you like. You always were closer to her than I. Maybe if things work out with you and this Eileen, she would want to live here with you."

"Irene."

"Irene," Calvin confirmed. "I can't stick around here where everyone has gotten to know me any longer. Sure, Doc Bergstrom must have noticed how I look, and even the doctors in Butte, but they were all aware of my work, and no one has said a word. I have to move away where no one knows the difference. It's the Waba, you know. The secret ingredient."

"I know," Ralph replied. "I had my suspicions."

Calvin stopped pacing and turned to him. "Why haven't you ever said anything?"

The frail old man stood and put his Chicago Cubs cap on his bald head. He smiled up at his longtime friend and boss and said, "Because I believe you are making a very large mistake, brother."

The men stared at each other in silence. Finally, Ralph straightened up and squared his shoulders. "I will take you up on your offer, about the house and land, I mean. Figure out what you want for rent; I have money saved up. I can afford it."

"No, Ralph," Calvin whispered. "The place is yours. I'll have my attorney take care of everything."

Ralph crossed the room on unsteady legs and held out his hand. Calvin stared at it for a moment, taking note of the papery skin and liver spots, then he took it in his own and shook it. He thought he might break the bones inside.

"I love you, Calvin," Ralph said. "Good luck."

Just like that, their working relationship, and their close friendship was over.

∞

Calvin found another home, this time in Oregon.

He looked at four different places, all of them outside of a small, yet self-sustaining town. The first three were nice, but everything about them reminded him of Elaina, from the carpet to the paint, to the garden plots outside. No, he had determined quickly. None of them would do.

All he wanted, or needed, for that matter, was a place with a single bedroom and a large enough area inside to put together a small, fully functional laboratory. He would stay in and work. He wouldn't make friends or mix with the locals for anything other than grocery shopping or business. After all, the last thing he needed was for people to start trying to get to know him.

It was the fourth and final house that he settled on. It was located thirty miles outside of a town called Hilton, and it was perfect. Small, unassuming, and extraordinarily private. He went ahead and got telephone and utility services hooked up, but he passed on the luxury of pay television. After all, he would never watch it. Instead, he purchased a small weather radio from a store in town. That way he would be on top of storms and the like, without having to waste any time and money on something he would never likely use anyway.

As for his lab, Calvin ended up deciding to use the only bedroom for that. He would sleep on the couch in the living room when he did sleep. He hadn't done much of that since losing Elaina, anyway. He made some minor changes, hooked up his burners and put in some countertops and storage space, as well as a single recliner to rest in, and it was complete. From there he moved in all of the years and years of records and notes, and Calvin Cooper was set.

It was time to get back to work.

The formula worked. Now his focus would be entirely on shrinking the dosage and making it easier to take. He would love to make it a one-time thing, a pill which could be ingested and forgotten about forever, one which stimulated age reversal and then continually maintained it, either forever for the user, or until they decided they wanted to stop. He would work on a supplement to go with the formula which could be taken to cease the effects of the formula at that time if so desired.

He would call the formula 'ElainaYouth.'

Next, Calvin set up accounts with the companies who provided him with his lab supplies, but he set them up under Elaina's name, and he paid with a credit card which had her name on it, one she had used while she was still alive. He wanted no curiosities, no questions, and most of all, no recognition on the part of delivery men or company salespeople if they happened to visit.

He was going to be careful.

So, Calvin got to work.

He knew it was the Waba which was the key to all of his goals and dreams. Now, all he had to do was begin testing it exclusively, and the best way he saw fit to do that was to hit the local animal shelter, just as he and Ralph had been doing toward the end. He would find an old dog and bring it home, and if things worked out the way Calvin was sure they would, the animal wouldn't be old for long.

He named the first dog 'Chip.' Chip was a worn out old border collie which had been found wandering on the side of the highway by animal control workers. He was emaciated and untrusting, but as soon as he met Calvin, he came directly out of his shell. For Calvin taking Chip in was a no-brainer.

Soon he was back to work, and he was completely submerged in his craft. He rose at the crack of dawn, fed and treated Chip with a fraction of a similar dose he and Ralph had given to other animals, and then he dove in. His main focus, at first, was the intense study of Waba. If he was going to lessen and empower ElainaYouth, he was going to have to know his secret ingredient inside out. It wasn't going to be enough just to trust its power; he needed to master it in its entirety.

He began to grow it once again, starting the small saplings in his tiny dining room, then replanting them in his fenced in backyard, away from prying eyes. He had some Waba paste and a bit of raw Waba with him when he moved to Oregon, as well as a couple of saplings, which he planted immediately after moving. As for the paste and raw material, Calvin used it sparingly and made sure it would last.

But things were not to go as smoothly or as easily as he hoped they would. Chip showed promise, but the change was extremely slow, and Calvin found himself having to adjust the dosage time and again. He also ended up having to purchase high powered fertilizer, then was distracted by having to improve on that. Otherwise, his trees would never be ready in time, and without the Waba he had nothing to work with.

Calvin Cooper's life consisted of tending Waba trees, treating Chip, and concentrating day and night on working with what he had, which was very little in that first couple of years. He wasn't worried, though. Once his trees began to get going, he would begin to fly, and before he knew it he would have ElainaYouth perfected, and it would be ready to use.

He would change the world.

CHAPTER 15

2021

"Here, boys!"

Calvin gave a piercing whistle, and the dog, which had been sniffing around a hole near the head of the driveway, turned quickly and gave his master his attention. His tail immediately began to wag out of control, and he ran, full-speed, back to the man who called himself 'Dad.' The man who had saved his life from the prison of the dog pound.

No sooner did Chip begin to run back to him than another dog, which had been hidden from sight by the large bushes running across the front yard, came around the corner, running right behind Chip. Calvin had gotten this one about a year after Chip. He was a mutt, so to speak, his species pretty unidentifiable, though Cal thought he was some type of terrier mix. His name was Monk, and he had been in far worse shape than Chip when Calvin picked him out and brought him home.

Monk had been beaten and horribly neglected by whoever had owned him. A couple of his legs had been broken, and he was barely able to move around. Treating Monk was fairly easy: he had pretty much perfected his 'doggie-dosage,' as he liked to call it when treating Chip, even though it took him quite some time to get that right. One of the most important things he had learned was that dosages would differ depending not only on the size of the patient, but also on how much damage had been done to them during the course of their life.

In the back, next to his Waba orchard, Calvin put in a kennel, which housed six dogs at any given time. On the other side, and up along the side of the house so it was out of the dogs' sight, was an enclosed area he had built for cats. For the last twenty-five years, he had toiled away on the ElainaYouth formula, treating cats and dogs, until he got it right.

He had also continued to take the formula himself, but even now, twenty-five years after moving to Oregon, he still found he had to ingest an insane amount of it just to maintain the age of his appearance. He looked to be just under forty, he guessed, which wasn't so bad. After all, he was ninety-eight years old. But he felt incredible; everything but his soul, anyway. That was hollow, lonely, and empty.

A day's worth of his formula, to maintain his looks and youthful feel, added up to nearly a quart, which he diluted in water and drank. Any less than that and he found he was a bit tired and sore the following day, and within a week he could see gray hairs creeping their way into his thick, black mane. But he couldn't complain; when he had first relocated, he was using nearly a gallon a day for self-maintenance, so progress was indeed being made.

Oh, but it was slow… so terribly slow.

But the years had flown, and here he was, in tip-top condition, so did it matter? Calvin decided it certainly did not. He had all the time in the world, according to his calculations.

Today he would be working on something new, something he stumbled across the day before by accident.

He had brought a new dog home, this one an old black lab with a white, aging muzzle. The dog, which he named Tuxedo, had terrible arthritis in all of his joints. It was so painful for the animal that he would lie in one spot, urinate or defecate, then crawl out of the mess to a cleaner spot.

Calvin had been breaking down the chemicals in a Waba tree which he had just harvested. But he noticed something he had never taken note of before: the core of the trunk. The very center. He had always worked with the bark, the leaves, and the wood pulp. It was very effective, but he had struggled to minimize the dosage over the years, of course.

But yesterday, he had continued cutting and delving into the trunk because he wanted to make the trees last even longer. He didn't want to have to harvest a second tree in only one week, but with all the animals he was treating, he would have to at the rate he was going. So he scraped and cut, getting even the smallest wood scraps, all the way to the core. It was black and gummy, and he had noticed it several times. Ralph had even conducted some experimentation and testing on the substance, but it had a chemical which was very close to sulfur, and Calvin had rejected its use for years. But yesterday, out of desperation, he actually worked it. He heated it up, separating and extracting, and what he came up with in his effort to stretch it out, was the purest form of extract he had come up with, ever.

He had rolled the goo up in a tubular shape and let it sit overnight. This morning, on waking, he had tasted a sample of it, and it had been terribly bitter, so he went back to the drawing board, and finally, he coated the tube with the original sweet Waba paste he had used for so many years. Not only was it now palatable as a chewable tablet, but it was also quite delicious.

But how would it work?

Tuxedo would be the one to help him figure that out.

Calvin put Chip and Monk in the house, where they played with chew toys to the sound of the radio. He went into his lab and removed a covered dish from the small refrigerator he kept there. He put the dish down and removed the lid.

There, before him, sat a long tube. It was red in appearance, a beautiful, pure red, much like the color of fruit punch. He bent over and inhaled deeply. It had a rich, fruity smell that brought a smile to his face. Next, Calvin picked up a clean scalpel from the countertop and cut a centimeter-thick slice from the tube. He noted thoroughly its appearance, smell, and calculated dosage, as well as the expected outcome, in his recordings before gently closing the notebook and lovingly patting its cover.

He would give the chewable tablet to Tuxedo.

Calvin would give one tablet per day to the animal, along with regular meals and water. Nothing more and nothing less. He didn't want to get his hopes up; for all he knew, it would be 'back to the drawing board' soon. But if it did work, he expected it to begin to show in about two weeks. He would bring Tuxedo into the house and make the other two dogs stay outside in the kennels during this time, just to keep the crippled old canine safe and sound during the initial stages of the treatment.

"Alrighty, kids," he said, clapping his hands together enthusiastically. "Let's head outside. You're gonna be visiting your pals for a while but never fear. I'll run you each and every day, you hear?"

The dogs jumped up and followed him out the door as if his pockets were full of kibble. He petted them and played with them for a few minutes before leading them back to the kennel. There, he put each of them in its own cubicle, and he gently fished Tuxedo out, picking him up carefully in his arms. The dog whined in pain and began to tremble almost violently.

"It's alright, buddy. It's going to be okay," he said soothingly. "You're going to come into the house with me for a while, okay? You'll like it there. It's warm and cozy, and I have lots of yummy treats for you."

Inside, Calvin had arranged an area in the corner of the living room for the dog. It had thick, fluffy blankets, a food, and water dish, and was stationed right next to an identical set up. That way Tuxedo could crawl to clean bedding if he messed, and Calvin could clean up after him easily and arrange another pallet of bedding for the next time.

He laid the poor dog down carefully, but the animal cried out anyway. Next, he stood up and went into his lab. He took the chewable tablet into his fingers gently, handling it as if it were made of glass. He held it up to the sunlight, which was shining through the window like a promise, and he smiled. Yes, Calvin Cooper had a good feeling about this. A good feeling indeed.

He approached Tuxedo, whose tail began wagging immediately. Calvin knelt by the dog and began to pet him with his right hand, and he held the tablet under the dog's nose with his left. The tail thumped harder as the dog sniffed at the small disk-shaped item.

"It's your yummy medicine, boy," Calvin told him. "It will make you feel all better, kiddo. I promise."

As if he understood English plainly, the dog popped his tongue out of his mouth and lapped the tablet a single time, drawing it into his mouth. He chewed only once, then gulped it down, and he followed this up by looking up at Calvin with his rheumy eyes for approval.

"Good job, Tux!" Cal enthused as he stroked the animal's fur. "Yes, that's a good boy! Now you rest. Dad has work to do."

Calvin returned to the lab, where he sliced the remainder of the Waba tube into tablets, and placed them, covered, back into the refrigerator. He began to record details in his book and, just as he had his entire life, Calvin Cooper lost track of time. He extracted, heated, and mixed. He peered through his microscope, noted, and peered some more. He went outside and treated and fed the animals, cleaned their kennels, and then turned his attention to the Waba orchard. Before he knew it, it was after nine at night, and his stomach threatened to turn on him. He was starving, and he was tired.

Calvin ate a bologna and cheese sandwich, which he chased with Waba water. Then he checked on Tuxedo, whom he expected to find on the clean palate, but the dog was still on the original one, sleeping soundly. His food dish was empty, and his water was nearly gone. Calvin smiled, glad the dog was comfortable in the house.

After making sure that the weather radio was on, Cal settled in on the couch, soft music coming from the radio. It was the sound of Bill Haley and the Comets, a band he had loved in his early thirties. They just don't make music like this anymore, he thought, then he quickly dozed off into a deep sleep.

∞

Calvin was lying on the soft grass, staring up at the broad leaves of a massive Waba tree. In his dream, it was one of his trees, one of the trees from the orchard, but for some reason, this one had grown incredibly fast, and it was five, no ten times larger than all the other trees there. He had lain down on the ground to take in its gigantic beauty, and to experience the full impact of the sight of it.

Now, as he lay there, smiling and cooing at the breathtaking plant, its limbs began to reach down, slowly for him. The sound he was making seemed to be attracting the plant, which obviously had a mind of its own: it could think! The limb closest to his face continued to get closer, closer, and even closer. It was covered with leaves, but when it was about five feet away one leaf in particular suddenly separated from the others, and it reached for him with effort and grace.

It lingered over his face, fluttering back and forth, but not whimsically. No, it was an intentional fluttering, as if it were trying to hypnotize him with its movements. Almost as if it were… teasing him.

Calvin began to smile, and a giggle escaped his lips. As soon as the sound left him, the leaf touched his face. It was gentle at first, and it tickled slightly, making him giggle even louder. It jerked away from him, then slowly came at him again. This time when it touched him, it was more insistent, brushing his cheek again and again, and the leaf was… wet.

Calvin's eyes flew open to see large brown ones staring back at him. He was surrounded by the smell of dog breath, and the reality of the wetness on his cheek was strong. He reached up and wiped his cheek off, his eyes clenched shut as he sat up on the edge of the couch.

"Tuxedo, yuck!" he exclaimed as he wiped at his cheek. Suddenly his mind cleared all at once, and he looked at the dog sitting next to him.

Tuxedo was seated on his haunches comfortably. His tail was thumping loudly on the floor, and he appeared to be smiling. His brown eyes were empty of pain and cloudiness, but what Calvin noticed above all else was the dog's muzzle.

It was completely black, not a stray white hair in sight.

"Tux?"

The early morning sun was streaming through the window, but none of it was shining on either of them. Calvin flipped the switch to the lamp on the end table, and it came on in a bright glare, illuminating everything around him. Calvin's eyes squinted in its brightness, but Tuxedo only began to wag his tail with more joy and insistence than before.

"Do you need to go potty, boy? Need to go outside?" He stared at the animal in disbelief as the tail began to wag out of control. Tuxedo suddenly jumped up on him, knocking him back against the couch, and he began licking Cal's face uncontrollably.

"Okay! Okay, let's go," he said, pushing the dog off of him.

As soon as he opened the front door, the dog bolted outside into the morning air. He ran in circles, sniffing everything in sight, not a sign of pain or discomfort in any of his movements or actions. Calvin's mouth hung open in disbelief. This can't be happening, he thought. I gave him only one tablet...

The animal lifted his leg and watered the trunk of an elm near the driveway before finding a spot near a bush, where he squatted for a bit. After that, he ran around the side of the house, toward the rear where the kennels were. Calvin had to run in his bare feet to catch up, dew covering his skin and making his feet icy cold. He found Tuxedo running up and down the length of the kennel, smelling each and every dog there. All of them began barking all at once, which set off the cats.

"Tux, we have to go in! Time to go in now!"

Immediately the dog followed him, and together they ran for the house. Once inside, Calvin sat on the couch and got the dog to take a sitting position on the floor next to him. He stared at the animal, its face cupped in his hand as he studied him.

"What the heck is going on, boy?" Calvin asked. "I told you that medicine would help, but I'll be damned..."

He studied the dog for another moment before running to the lab for his book and pen. For the next hour, he examined the canine, who was in seemingly perfect health and had the energy of a young dog. Calvin was not only dumbfounded, but he was also overwhelmed.

When the hour was up, Calvin fed the dog and then went out to tend to the other animals. He couldn't stop smiling; he was so excited and pleased he thought he might burst. He even talked to his Elaina, speaking up at the sky and telling her all about it.

But then concern came over him. If that happened overnight, he couldn't risk giving the animal another tablet. He may wake up to a puppy! No, he was going to hold off on giving Tuxedo any more treatments until he noticed the dog regressing. That was the only way to perfect the new tablets and their dosage.

But he did give one to all the other animals and split the tablets in two for the felines. He fed and watered them all, then fetched his saw from the shed. He went to the largest of the Waba trees, and Calvin Cooper spent the next forty-five minutes cutting it down and slicing the trunk into six-inch sections.

He forgot to eat or even dress. Instead, Calvin spent the entire day making up another tube-shaped portion of ElainaYouth. He was obsessed, and he couldn't believe all of his dreams were finally becoming a reality. But he wouldn't celebrate, not yet. He would monitor all the animals for a week, at which time he would begin taking the new dosage himself. Then he would spend yet another week monitoring both the animals and himself. If all worked out, if he succeeded, then and only then would he let himself celebrate.

So, once again, Calvin dove in headfirst and shut out the rest of the world.

∞

By the end of the first week after Tuxedo's overnight transformation, Calvin had a very strong feeling that the animal was completely maintained.

As a matter of fact, by the end of day two, he seemed younger than ever, and Cal was seriously worried that he had overdone it. Had he given the dog so much Waba that time would continue to reverse to the point of pre-existence? The man couldn't sleep or eat, he was so concerned, but by day three, Tux balanced out, and he remained stable from there on out, not getting younger, but not aging or regressing either.

It seemed that Calvin had done it.

He had planned to begin the formula himself at that point but decided to wait and monitor the other animals as well. It wouldn't hurt to watch them all for a full two weeks. As a matter of fact, Calvin felt it was a necessary obligation. So, the man pitched a tent outside near the kennels and began the monitoring process. He woke every hour, on the hour, to check them. He maintained a close eye and noted everything from the size of their stools to the quickness of their reflexes.

And sure enough, after two weeks, each and every one of them was as healthy and strong as they were the day after the treatment. He was beside himself. On day fourteen, after completing his notes for the day, he unlocked the kennels, and all the animals came to him, running, pouncing, and jumping. Calvin Cooper fell to the ground, and all of them surrounded him, licking him and loving him. Shockingly they didn't fight or fuss with each other. It was as if they knew what he had done, and they refused to give him any trouble.

It was that day that he took the tablet for himself.

He ate it quickly, his heart pounding and his hands trembling. He had cut this tablet just a little thicker, adjusting it for his weight. He wrote extensive notes, even recording his thoughts and feelings. He was terribly nervous; what if he woke to find he was twelve years old again? He didn't think that would happen. He hoped the dosage he gave himself would be appropriate for age maintenance, and that was all. No more, and no less.

Tomorrow, when he woke, if all were well, he would allow himself to celebrate. He would get in the car and take a drive to Hilton. There he would buy a bottle of champagne, the kind he and Elaina used to love, and he would buy a television set and some rabbit ears. It would be set up, and then he, Chip, Monk, and Tuxedo would have dinner together and watch some television like he and his wife would do every now and then. That was how he would celebrate his victory, the perfection of ElainaYouth.

As he settled down on the couch for the night, his mind raced. It took him literally hours to shut off enough to doze, and when he finally did sleep, his dreams were filled with ageless people from every decade and every year in the history of the world. He stood on the top of a mountain, his beautiful bride, still alive, by his side, as the Earth's population cheered and chanted his name.

Yes, Calvin Cooper had finally found success, and he knew it in his heart.

R.W.K. Clark

CHAPTER 16

He woke with a start and stared frantically around the living room. Had it all been a dream? He adjusted his eyes to the dimly sunlit room and looked around until he found Tuxedo. The dog was right next to the couch, lying down but wide awake.

"How goes it, Tux ol' boy?" he asked.

The dog jumped right up and approached him, tail going crazy. No, it was real. It was all real.

"Let's get you outside," he said, patting the dog's head. "I'll check on all the others, then I need to run to town, okay?"

He put his loafers on, grabbed his book and pen, and opened the front door, letting the black lab run out ahead of him. As the dog did his business, Calvin opened the book to take notes, and suddenly remembered something very important, something it seemed he had forgotten briefly.

He had taken a tablet.

Calvin dropped his book and pen on the ground, Tuxedo forgotten and ran back into the house. He made a beeline for the bathroom, where he flung the door open and flipped on the overhead light. Then he positioned himself in front of the mirror, his head down. Calvin took a single deep breath and looked.

At first, he could see no change, but then he really, really looked. His hair was a bit longer, and his eyes a bit clearer. He noticed that the minor lines he had around his eyes were completely gone, and his eyebrows were bushier, as they had been when he was in his early to mid-thirties. But what he noticed most of all was the fact that he had no glasses on, and he could see as clearly as if his eyes were brand new.

He had always worn glasses to help him read, at least since the last year of high school, but when he was thirty-nine, he had to get glasses for nearsightedness as well. But now, here he stood, looking at his reflection, and he didn't have to strain in the slightest.

He looked to be thirty to thirty-two years of age.

Calvin jumped up and down right there in the bathroom. "You did it, Old Man!" he shouted into the mirror. "You really have done it, you crazy so-and-so!"

Just as quickly as he became excited, he calmed down. "Now all you have to do is be sure it is going to stop." He pointed his forefinger into the mirror. "But celebrate, you will!"

He fed and checked on all the animals, completing the morning notes for them. Next, he let Tuxedo go into the kennel with the other dogs to play while he went into the house. He made fried eggs, sausage, hashed browns, and toast. This had been his favorite breakfast in younger years, one that he could've eaten for any meal of the day. But he had eventually passed it up completely when he became… obsessed.

"How long has it been, Cal?" he asked himself as he flipped his eggs. "A good thirty years or more, wouldn't you say? Well, today you eat like a movie star, you handsome devil, you. You deserve it, Old Man!"

Calvin completely cleaned his plate, sopping up the remaining yolk with his toast and drinking a cold glass of milk down in a single pour. Next, he showered and dressed, combing his hair with care. Time to go into town and do a bit of television shopping. He would also get himself a T-bone, a bag of potatoes, and a couple of ears of corn. He would make a dinner he wouldn't soon forget.

Soon he was driving to Hilton, humming to himself. He didn't listen to regular radio much anymore because they didn't play much music he cared for, and he never had been a fan of the news. Humming oldies was good enough for him. He wasn't picky, after all.

In Hilton, he found a large shopping store called FunMart. It was massive, and when he saw the people milling in and out of the place, he nearly became overwhelmed by trepidation. It seemed to be just too much.

"Okay, look Old Man," he said to himself. "You have earned this, and there is nothing to be afraid of, so get moving."

Once inside, he was nearly overcome once again. People rushed here and there, bumping into each other without so much as a simple "sorry" or "excuse me." It seemed everyone had someplace to be, but no one was going anywhere. Children screamed at their parents, who stood there pretending it wasn't happening. Others talked to their companions behind their hands, whispering and pointing at others, making obvious fun.

The world was a very, very rude place, at least in Hilton, Oregon anyway.

He bucked himself up once again and began to follow signs with arrows that pointed him to 'Electronics.' He assumed that was where he would be able to purchase a new television. He was a scientist after all; what else would they sell there?

But when he arrived at that department, his breath was knocked from his body. The televisions were large and flat, with huge screens. All of them had a different program playing, and the sound was turned up on each, making it nearly impossible to discern one show from another. He stood, confused and frightened. Nothing was as he remembered it, and nothing was as he anticipated, not in the slightest.

"Can I help you sir?"

Calvin jumped slightly and turned around. "Um, yes, I think so, anyway." He turned to the young lady in a red smock. She had a silver dot on the side of her nose, and her hair was blond with hot pink on the bottom. Calvin knit his brow and tried not to stare. "I wanted to buy a television, but I haven't had one in some time, and I'm a bit confused."

"Did you want a large one or a smaller one?" She gestured toward the sets with her hand as she spoke.

Calvin looked at each of them. The small ones

seemed too small, and larger ones were too much to take in. After a moment, he pointed at one that was right in between size-wise. "I think that looks about right. What do you think?"

"Whatever suits your taste, Mister," she replied as she grabbed a box from a lower shelf beneath all the sets. She grabbed an empty cart that was sitting deserted and put the box inside of it. "There you go, sir. You can check out in the front of the store."

"So, I just take it home, plug it in, and hook up the rabbit ears," he said. "It should be fine, right?"

A confused look came over her face. "Rabbit ears?" She stared at him, waiting for an answer, then her face cleared and she smiled. "You mean those old antennas? We don't use those anymore, not for years. You'll need a digital box and antenna. It has been a while for you, hasn't it?"

She started to walk away, then turned around and looked at him, amused. "Follow me," she said. "I'll get you what you need, okay?"

He grabbed the cart and began to trail after her, feeling completely out of his element. Two aisles down, she grabbed a couple of smaller boxes and held them up to him. She smiled at the look on his face.

"Okay, when you hook up your television at home, all you have to do is follow the directions on these, and soon you'll be up and running." She put both of the boxes in his cart. "Now listen: if you have any problems, all you have to do is call the customer support telephone numbers on the boxes; both the antenna and the digital box are from the same manufacturer. Someone there will be able to walk you through the process."

Calvin looked down at the items, his mind a jumbled mess. "Can't I just get a TV like, you know, the boxy kind? Don't you carry any of those?"

The girl's smile faded as she realized he was serious. She put her hand on his arm and said, "It really has been awhile. No one sells those anymore, sir. The government mandated that everything go digital. You know, since the World Trade was attacked by terrorists."

The World Trade attacks? Terrorists? What the heck was this girl talking about? Calvin was beginning to sweat. He wanted to ask, but she was already looking at him as though he were an alien from outer space.

"Oh, that's right," he said with a fake chuckle. "I work a lot, and only now do I have time to watch a little television. I guess I just forgot."

Now the girl smiled again, a look of relief joining the grin. "No problem. Like I said, you can check out up front at the registers, or I can do it back here if you prefer."

He nodded. "That would be better, I think."

Within twenty minutes, Calvin had his boxes in his car, and he was sitting behind the wheel breathing in and out as if trying to overcome hyperventilation. He would have been out sooner, but it took him ten full minutes just to find his car. Now he just had to get to the grocery store. His groceries had been delivered since he moved to Oregon, so he hoped food stores hadn't changed too much.

They hadn't. Calvin was able to get the food he wanted quickly. When it came time to check out, he had to have help with the card machine, just like at the FunMart, so he just let the cashier handle it for him. By the time he was headed home, he had made a solemn promise to himself that he wouldn't do that anytime again soon.

He arrived home shortly before noon and set about hooking up the set. The instructions were simple for him, fortunately, as he had always been good at steps, thanks to his scientific mind. By one he had the set on, channels scanned, and everything running smoothly.

He decided to let the television play while he worked. He was going to begin focusing on some kind of antidote for ElainaYouth, something that could be used to counteract an out-of-control dosage. He may even need it; he wouldn't know for a couple of days.

Before he started, he checked on all the animals once again and fed them, then noted, with joy, that nothing had changed. Over two weeks and everything looked more than good to go. He could head inside and work with a clear mind.

He set the television on a channel which was broadcasting the news and turned up the volume. It was high time he got in sync with the world again, and that fact hit him hard after his experience at the FunMart. He'd never been so damned confused in all of his life, and it was his own doing. No, it was time to play catch up.

So he began to work, reading a bit and listing compounds that would counteract the chemicals in the Waba. It would be a long, arduous journey, so he was eager to start quickly. After all, it wouldn't do to actually harm someone with ElainaYouth.

But as he worked, his mind caught the fringes of what was being said on the television. Each commercial, each announcement, and each news broadcast over the next few hours was completely clear and audible. Calvin couldn't wholly concentrate on the task at hand.

And to be honest, he was beginning to get more than a little sick and frightened.

"Ten were killed in Coos Bay today when a lone gunman opened fire in McBurger's..."

"Teen pregnancy is at an all-time high..."

"A terrorist attack reportedly killed fifty people..."

"The man said he beat his wife to death because his steak was cold..."

"Eight found dead at Ohio State University..."

This went on and on and on, and by four, Calvin felt sick to his stomach. He gave up on his work for the day and turned the set off. He would begin his supper, and then he would find an evening movie to watch, one that made him laugh. He checked the animals and began to cook.

By six-thirty he had eaten, dedicating his special meal to his Elaina. After he finished the dishes, he went out and got his three pals, Chip, Monk, and Tux, and brought them in the house. He chose a movie called

'The Cons,' and settled in, dogs all around.

But the film was horrible. It was violent and sexually graphic, and the women in the movie were nearly naked. They had horrible mouths and degraded the men they were with. Children ran around like adults, smoking, drinking, and having sex.

Calvin found himself on the verge of tears.

By the time it was over, he had decided to watch the evening news to get his mind off the horrors of the movie. He thought it would be a good distraction, a way to get back into touch with reality. He thought it would help him sleep easier.

But it was worse than ever. Politicians were on drugs. They lied, cheated, and stole. The government was helping terrorists, and teachers were having sex with their students in junior high schools. Prostitutes roamed the streets, and mothers murdered their own babies.

The world was in chaos.

By ten, Calvin shut off the set completely. He sat in the light of the lamp on the end table, the dogs sleeping at his feet, snoring lightly in the quietness of the house. He stared straight ahead, tears running down his face, his mind a mass of confused, pained grey matter.

He had created something that was supposed to change the world. It was supposed to give people back their youthfulness and agility, their zest for life. He had always planned to perfect it and sell it, giving anyone and everyone the option to be young, beautiful, and healthy forever.

But now he knew: he could not do this with a clear conscious.

It would be criminal to spring Elaina Youth on the world for all to have access to. The evil souls running around today would be able to live forever, hurting others, raping the innocent, murdering and pillaging, with no thought at all to what they were doing. No… he just couldn't.

On that day in 2021, a thirty-year-old looking ninety-eight year old named Calvin Cooper, who had dedicated his whole life to the cause of making life better, watched his life crumble before his very eyes.

After all these years, he finally knew exactly what Elaina and Ralph had meant…

CHAPTER 17

2041

Nothing would ever counteract the Waba, and nothing would ever rid the world of the evil in the hearts of men.

Calvin Cooper sat in the darkness of his laboratory in his Hilton home. The sunlight crept through the window blinds, revealing the dust as it danced and settled here and there on the beakers and burners and notebooks. Calvin had touched none of those things in twenty years.

His eyes glanced to the left, toward the shelves at the end of the dust-covered countertops, but they were the only parts of him that moved at all. The rest of his body sat in the old recliner, still and motionless. His eyes glanced, and they settled on a jar with six tube-shaped sticks inside. A paper sticker on the front of the jar read 'ElainaYouth,' written in cursive letters.

Next to it was another jar. Its paper sticker read 'Antidote.' It held nothing, and a fly buzzed lazily around it.

His eyes shifted forward again, and he sighed.

His mind wandered back to Boston University, and

the day he ran headlong into a beautiful blond coed, a girl so full of sparkle and life that she had blinded him. She had teased him about lunch and sweet gelatin, and that simple statement had proven to be groundbreaking for him.

He thought about the look on her face that night at the awards ceremony when she saw Clara kissing him. The pain in her eyes could be felt by him from clear across the room. He would never in a million years dream of causing any pain to his dear Elaina, yet there it was. To that day he still felt sorrow over the misunderstanding.

He thought about the look on her face in the moonlight later that night, the look she gave him when he proposed. He recalled her spunk when she wanted to go back in and dance with him for that red-head to see. The memory made his lips smile, and his heart bleed.

Next, he recalled the electric shaver Elaina had given him for their twentieth anniversary, and how happy she was for him to be able to shave himself, finally, since he never looked in the mirror. Also recalling when they got home to find Ralph, panicky and fretting because the lab had been burglarized. Additionally how understanding and loyal she had been all during the charges that followed and the court proceedings.

Their move to Twixt, and Maddie the horse, his first successful experiment with the youth formula. Noah Carter! Oh, how she took care of that man, and how she had presented him to Cal and Ralph when he suddenly was… healed. Her joy over her husband's success. How she had loved him! And love like that, well, it just doesn't happen twice.

Then Switzerland. They saw all the best sights, all the things she had daydreamed about and spoken of. On the night of their anniversary, she had passed out as they danced, and he had feared for her life. He made her go to the doctor, and he found himself wishing he never had, but he knew it wouldn't have changed anything. One simply cannot trick fate, one simply cannot cheat death.

Everyone died. He knew that now. Everyone except him and a large group of dogs and cats…

She had refused the formula. She didn't want to live forever, only the number of days God had set for her. Neither had Ralph, his trusty friend, and assistant. Ralph had said, "I believe you are making a terrible mistake…" Oh, Calvin had no idea what that really meant at the time, but now he knew all too well that both Elaina and Ralph were much wiser to the things of life than he ever dreamed of being. He had been fooled by the bubble of ignorance which he had wrapped around himself. He had painted himself into a blissful little corner where he believed that life could be easily changed by living forever and being beautiful forever.

But now Calvin Cooper knew that beauty was so much more than skin deep.

The television set was the gateway to the things nightmares were made of. It was murder and death, hatred and destruction. It pushed its opinions and perspectives into the homes and lives of all who sat like zombies before it, and soon people were killing each other, stealing from each other, and hating. It was a horrid, terrible gadget, but as far as the state of the world was concerned?

It was right, and the world was so very, very bad.

He had come so far in achieving his goals. Yes, he certainly had done it, in spades. Give him a sick, old dog or cat, or even a man, and he would turn it all around. If their heart was pure, he could give them hope. Hope to fix broken relationships and hearts. But even old Noah Carter had known, even in the midst of a repaired father-daughter relationship that life was never meant to be lived forever. Not on this forsaken mudball called Earth, anyway.

So what was it for? Calvin, for most of his life, had honestly had no idea. He thought he did, but he had been wrong. It wasn't about being beautiful or eternally healthy. It wasn't about living forever. It was about heartache and pain and the lessons which could be gleaned from such. It had taken him more than his share of life to figure that out. Even his beloved Elaina could not teach that lesson to him, in her life or her death.

He was a stubborn, narrow-minded man.

Now he sat here gazing around at a lifetime of work that had proven to be worthless. Human beings were not equipped for the responsibility of eternity. Not on this planet or anywhere else, for that matter.

His heart ached over what that demon television had taught him.

He had turned on that television set a few times, and every time all there was to see and hear was a terror. As a matter of fact, he had panicked and began to try, with all his might, to find an antidote for the formula which he had so blindly taken. He wanted nothing more than to age and die, to join his wife as soon as possible. He wanted to remember an easier, more peaceful time. A time before the hate…

But those times were gone, and he couldn't leave with them.

There was no antidote to find. Calvin had worked and worked, toiled and slaved, but nothing. It had been twenty years since he finalized his success with ElainaYouth, and… nothing.

Not even the dogs or cats would die, and they were too stupid to know better. Calvin hadn't even considered their welfare. Every owner they would ever have would die, and they would be left, alone, forever. He had done each of them a grave injustice, and that was an understatement.

Finally, two years ago, he put an ad in the Hilton Herald for the dogs, all of which ended up finding new homes. The cats were another story; no one wanted them. They still wandered around his property, and he would put food out for them daily. He hated himself for what he had done. To the dogs, to the cats, and to himself.

Now he sat in his chair, and he was resigned as far as what he would do.

He would never be able to adjust, never be able to

join the world around him. His heart ached with that truth, and he couldn't stop the pain. He thought, maybe I should take another wife. Maybe I should start over.

But she would die someday, and that would be too painful. No, I cannot love another woman. Calvin hadn't aged a second in the last twenty years. No. He couldn't, wouldn't go through that pain again, and he still held Elaina sacred to his heart. He hated himself for not spending every waking day with Elaina in lieu of working on this formula.

He had to decide: he would start to live, or he would die. What would it be? Well, he had made up his mind.

So, in the dust and sunlight, Calvin Cooper looked down with his perfect thirty-year-old vision and stared at the loaded gun in his hand.

Yes, it was the only way to be free of the pain... so he stood and put the gun into the waistband of his pants. He picked up a container of gasoline from the floor next to the chair, and he began to pour it on everything in the lab. He poured it throughout the house, in every corner in every room.

No one would ever, ever discover or use ElainaYouth.

He stood at the front door and lit the match. Then, Calvin turned his back on that house and made his way through the backyard and into the Waba orchard. He leaned his back against the largest tree, the one in the middle, the one he assumed had infiltrated his dreams. He sat back, smiled, and put the gun to his head.

Calvin Cooper then pulled the trigger...

ENTREATY

This book was made possible by reviews from readers like you. Reviews fuel my creativity. If you enjoyed this novel, I implore you to please write a review and share your experience on the retailer's website. The livelihood for authors is entirely dependent on reviews, and I must say, it is the largest obstacle as a struggling author that I have encountered. Please tell a friend, tell a loved one about this read. With your help, I will be one step closer to overcoming this obstacle. In return, I thank you from the bottom of my heart, and sincerely appreciate your time and effort.

Humbled, with gratitude,

R.W.K. Clark

ABOUT THE AUTHOR

I am a father of two beautiful children, Jon and Kim. They are my motivating forces; they are the lighthouse in this vast ocean. In my life, they are the air that I breathe; they are the oasis in this desert of uncertainty. They are my greatest joy in life and my number one priority. I have a long list of hobbies, and I attribute that to my lust for life! I like to surround myself with positive people, who share the same interests. Family values, the arts, outdoors, nature, and travel are tops on my list. I embrace attending cultural and artistic events because I believe dramatic self-expression is the window to the soul. I wear my heart on my sleeve, and I still believe in chivalry, and I always treat people the way I want to be treated.

www.rwkclark.com